Faith's Shelter

A Tale of Love, Lust, Grace, and Redemption

Christopher Hamilton

Cover design by E. A. Logan

Character art by T. L. Combs

Dedication

Dedicated to those who love God,

And were wounded in His house.

Thank You

THANK YOU

To Pastors Anthony and Danielle,

We did it again. Thanks for making this happen.

To E. A. Logan,

Thanks for being my friend, even when I'm in author overdrive.

And most of all, to The One whose steadfast love is eternal,

Thank you for never forsaking the work of Your hands.

Act I

Chapter 1

Picture this: a late-spring day, in Ocala, Florida. In a lush green space within the heart of the city, the sounds of laughter and cheer abound, echoing to the clear blue sky.

In a time before the world shut down, the people of the city freely gathered. Amidst lawn games, an outdoor music stage with folding chairs populating the seating area, fresh buttered popcorn, balloon animals, and the great, smoky tent where the barbeque grills were churning out labors of love, stood The First Pentecostal Church of Ocala, a towering sandstone beacon, head-and-shoulders, as it were, above other edifices in the area.

At the beep of a walkie-talkie, the door from the church kitchen opened, and a raspy-yet-strong voice called out into the daylight:

"Viorica, we have more guests coming!" Sister Jenkins radioed across the field. "Could you collect their money?"

Viorica handed her serving tongs to Sister Michelle with a smile and took off from the barbeque serving platter, as fast as her kitten heels would allow, across the field, across the blacktop parking lot to the welcome booth.

What had Viorica sitting upright in her bed that morning, before her alarm even went off, was the feeling that she would touch destiny. She couldn't put her finger on it, but she found herself expecting that God would show up today with something she needed.

Retouching her wind-tossed, hip-length black hair back into an up do, and warming up her brightest smile, she began welcoming the newcomers to the picnic. Eight people from the community in total were waiting.

She had been going full speed ever since her feet hit the floor at 6 a.m. The sweat she had worked up was making her clothes cling to her "curses", as Sister Jenkins jokingly said. She ignored the lingering glances of the men, and expertly adjusted her new sun dress and under-tee to their proper, modest position.

She dutifully took her place at the booth with a smile as bright as the overhead sun.

"Welcome, glad you're here," she found herself saying, over and over. "Welcome, hope ya'll have a great time", and "be sure to come see us again Sunday morning!" She handed out wristbands, welcoming those who paid for the meal, and those who freely came to enjoy the event, with equal enthusiasm.

Months had been spent planning, organizing, detailing, and working night and day to make sure the annual Women's Ministry Picnic was befitting its reputation as the biggest community event of the year. She had been side-by-side with Sister Jenkins through every stage of the project, making sure it was a fine-tuned machine.

She was both dreading the impact on her sleep schedule once this was all over, while reveling in the pressure of the moment. Destiny, she decided, would have to wait. God would have to work around the agenda they had spent months crafting. There were things on the timetable that needed to get *done*.

She was looking down, quickly recounting money and tallying the meal tickets on a sheet of paper when the last person in line approached.

"Hi! Welcome to the picnic!" she said, keeping her tone at an even level of cheerfulness.

The responding voice inexplicably made her shudder, ever so slightly.

"Why, thank you. And who might you be?"

"Viorica," she said, correcting a small mistake on the sheet and extending her hand before looking up. "Strange name, I know, but you can call me..."

Her voice stopped as she met his eyes. She was expecting another kindly, middle-aged gentleman from the deep and polite tone she heard.

The reality in front of her—a tall, clean-shaven, handsome rogue with a disarming smile and perfectly kept rich brown hair—left her completely stunned.

Her split-second impression was that he was *too* perfect. From his meticulous hair down to his choice of shirt; obviously chosen to highlight his abs, which were a work of art. His skin carried a light bronzing, like her own, that spoke to some distant, exotic heritage. His eyes were a window to a warm soul, belying their icy blue and steel appearance.

He smiled wider, leaning forward. She blinked several times in a row before she realized he was waiting for her to finish her sentence. She managed to regain her composure by the help of the Lord.

"Vee," she said simply. "Most people call me that. Vee."

At that, he exhaled and relaxed, as if his entire body were anticipating hearing what she had to say.

"Well, Viorica, it's great to meet you. My name's Archer." He took her hand as mildly, as one takes a crystal goblet, and gave the slightest of warm grips. She hurried to say something before her face turned red.

"A pleasure to meet you. Are you from around here?"

"I'm not," he responded. "Just moved to the area, in fact. And I'm suddenly *very* glad I decided to come today."

With that, it was done. It was as if the sun suddenly brightened and turned up the heat ten more degrees as her face went into full blush. She hurried to find a suitable reaction: she coughed lightly, shuffled papers, and looked down at a pile of cash as if it were scurrying around the table.

Through it all, he still saw and smiled even wider than before.

Darn it.

"Nice to meet you Archer," she said, gathering all the cash and the first pile of paper that she hoped was significant. "Enjoy the picnic."

She was off, dashing toward the crowd near the grills again. She imagined it wouldn't be as hot over there.

Children ran and played in the sunshine with the sheer, simple joys of life and youth. The adults socialized among themselves and ate their money's worth of the generous spread. The church masterfully worked the crowd, engaging with the community, building friendships, and sharing the love of Jesus Christ to anyone who would lend an ear.

Viorica dropped off the cash and papers from the welcome booth before going out to run to and fro. She found ways to help wherever she could, but her priority was made clear: meet the people and be an ambassador for Christ. So, between breaking down tables as they were no longer needed, cleaning up one section of the church's two acres at a time, and keeping the food and beverages flowing, she let loose her smile once again and purposed in her heart to be a vessel.

She felt like she was failing. Miserably. It was like the Holy Spirit that normally empowered her to be a witness was silent, and the only thing she could think about was *him*.

Everywhere she went, she would spot him out the corner of her eye, no matter which way she turned. Worse yet, she knew that he saw her, and she knew that he knew that she knew he was looking at her.

It was too much. It was entirely too hot, even for a Florida gal, and she had too much to do. She congenially broke off from the stammering, empty conversation she was having with Lois, the visiting Florida State University student, and began looking around for a place to hide.

To her alarm, Archer spotted her from across the field and began making his way toward her.

She could see his lady-killing smile from here. *'Not today, satan. Not today.'*

She broke into something close to a run towards the church building, where Sister Jenkins and the rest of the Women's Ministry were gathering.

"Ok, so far we're doing good ladies!" Alloise Jenkins was calling out. Her voice held her trademark rasp with a hint of a Southern twang from many years ago.

"Let's keep things moving along. We want to engage as many of the guests as we can and get them to church Sunday! If you're not witnessing to someone, or praying them through, get this yard clean. I'm not trying to be here all night!"

Alloise had a complexion that consistently remained mild brown in the Florida sun. She was a wise and beautiful woman, barely in her 60's but her pure white hair, ever-increasing wrinkles, and jaundiced eyes made her appear far older.

The ladies filed out. Sister Jenkins was seated on a foldout chair when Viorica came up behind and lightly wrapped her arms around her shoulders. Without looking up from her small stack of papers Alloise patted Viorica on the arm.

"Are you staying out of trouble?" she asked. Viorica smiled and shrugged.

"Mostly," she said. She pulled up a chair beside her. Without a word, Sister Jenkins handed her half the stack.

Receipts from purchasing the day's supplies, she noted. Vee instantly set to logging them for the church bookkeepers.

"Did you get around to the college students?" Alloise asked. Her hands were lightly trembling as she moved papers in a method that made sense only to her and a few other people.

"I did...for a little." Viorica cleared her throat and hoped Alloise would drop the issue.

She didn't.

"Please tell me you made a connection. We need more university students."

"I know, ma, I know. I really tried."

Sister Jenkins stopped what she was doing to raise an eyebrow at her. "But?"

"But," she went on, "I was...distracted...a little. I don't think I'm on my game today."

"Vee, let me tell you something," Alloise sat forward, nearly on the edge of her seat. "This is important. Not only is it important for those young people to find Christ and change their lives, but it's major for the church. We *need* young blood around here, and the best way to do that is to make connections with university students. The more the better. I *trusted you* with making that happen today."

Viorica fumbled on some figures of her running tally. She scratched out her mistake and started back-tracking. "I know! I promise I did my best.

Odd day, that's all. Besides, I think the girl, Lois, I talked to is really hungry for God—"

"But did you let her know she can come here and be filled?" Viorica didn't have an answer, so she focused back on her math.

Alloise took her hand. "There's more than that, too," she said, her voice going quieter. She was out of 'leader' mode and into 'mother' mode. "You need a win. You need a victory under your name when the board starts considering my replacement. If you're gonna take over Women's Ministry when I'm gone—"

Viorica instantly gripped her hand with both of hers. "Don't you talk like that, ma. You don't. You're not going anywhere, anytime soon. I'll have plenty of time to worry about taking over Women's Ministry. You just focus on getting better."

Alloise smiled, half proud, half sad. "Girl, you're so sweet. But you listen to me: even if God heals me head to foot, I'm too old to lead this ministry where we need to go. The church board is going to hold a vote in the fall."

Viorica's eyes went wide. "Why so soon?"

"I'm stepping down."

She felt like her heart skipped a beat, and not in a good way. "That's *too* soon," she said. "I have so much I need to do...I haven't been back in the church long enough!"

"I know, girl, I know," Alloise gripped her hands now. "That's why we need to put your name out there. You have to show you're a better fit for leading the ministry. Sister Hardy has had her eye on it, and now she has her whole family supporting her."

Viorica's face turned even paler than it had been. "How am I supposed to compete with that?" she asked. She felt like she was losing control, and hated that it was showing in her voice.

Alloise pulled her into a hug. Viorica laid her head on her shoulder, and let the tears silently fall. She had worked too hard, come *too far*, to lose now.

After a minute, Alloise lifted Viorica's head and wiped the tears away with her sleeve. "Listen to me, Vee: I already told you what to do, and how to do it. The plan is the same; you remember what it is?"

"Focus on the youth," she said right away. "Build the youth and young adult population, and let them see that I can be a leader."

"Right! Because you *can*, Viorica!" Sister Jenkins rarely used her full name. Whenever she did, she knew it was serious; 99% of the time it happened when she was trying to encourage her.

"With your determination, your confidence, your drive? You can be the leader that all the young girls look up to, and even these older women would follow you! That's why I've been investing in you! Emma could do a good job, so could Michelle, but they would only keep things the way they are. We need to grow if it's going to survive when we're all dead and gone. Nobody wants a museum for church."

"How can we do that before the vote?" Vee wiped the remaining tears off her own face. The only person she could stand to see her crying was Sister Jenkins, and barely even then. It was time to pull it together.

"Step one was 'make connections at the picnic'! What happened to you, anyway? You *never* let any ol' thing distract you."

Viorica let loose a sigh. She knew where this was going to end up. "Just...a lot of things. Trying to do too much, I guess. I don't think this dress is modest enough for me. The men were staring, the women were staring, it's burning up outside..."

"Uh-huh. What's the real reason?"

Another sigh. "So there was this guy..."

She blushed again as Alloise's face instantly bloomed in a grin. "No! Don't...it's not like that, ma! He just showed up, and he kept...*smiling* at me!"

She gave up as Alloise melted away in strained laughter, holding her side and reaching one hand out. Vee took her hand and helped her stand to her feet. She was a confused mash of concern, guilt, and embarrassment.

"I think...I think I saw," Alloise said, trying to regain her breath and fight through the laughter. "I saw him. That boy with the nice hair and his little brother's shirt?"

"Sounds like him." They began walking towards the door.

Alloise gripped her arm and halted short in her tracks. Viorica stumbled a little from the abrupt stop.

"Viorica, listen," she was still smiling, a mere step away from full laughter, but her eyes and her tone were stone-cold serious. "Sometimes God has plans that are completely the opposite of our own. It's fine to take a detour that God's leading you on."

Viorica frowned. "I don't know about that, ma..."

"Girl! Trust me! It's about time for you to go on and get married to a nice, handsome young man. The ministry'll be here once you get settled."

"What if somebody else takes over while I'm off getting married?"

Alloise shrugged. "Then it was never God's will to begin with."

"Ma, we prayed on this. I've done so much fasting they could take out half my stomach and I wouldn't notice. I know it's God's will for me!"

"But you don't know *when.*"

She had her on that one.

After she let the silence linger, Alloise started forward again. Viorica opened the door and led her back out into the Florida sun.

Once Alloise was settled, Viorica re-focused on her mission: find Lois and make that connection. There was still a sizable crowd, but noticeably less than it was half an hour ago. People here and there were packing up and taking off, while a few stayed behind to mingle, get seconds on barbeque, or learn more about the church.

She stopped by the pit to check on the workers. They had all the food ready for the taking, and were busy cleaning the grills and utensils for storage.

She spotted Emma speaking with Michelle. The three young women considered themselves friends, and sometimes friendly rivals in the running for head of the Women's Ministry. It was an odd dynamic, being in competition for a ministry, but it seemed to work; none of them tried to undercut the others, at the very least.

Emma Hardy was a living spark, 5'6" and strawberry blonde hair that fell below her knees, a testament to her life spent in an Apostolic church. With her dynamic personality, she was practically the face of the church when it came time for outreach in the city. That same personality also helped her win her husband Wendle, a quiet construction worker who would rather disappear into a crowd than be in the center of it.

Michelle Tabor was the polar opposite. Taller, dark brown hair past her waist, but her personality was far more reserved. She was a quiet introvert, unless she was in a group she was comfortable with, and that usually consisted of people who grew up in church with her.

But, as things stood, only one of them could be the head of the ministry. Hence, the subtle tension that grew stronger the closer Alloise got to retiring.

"Sisters, how'd it all go?" Vee asked. They smiled at her.

"I'd say it was a success," Emma said. She was watching Vee closely. "But from what I saw, you'd *definitely* agree."

Vee blushed again as she shook her head. She knew what Emma was referring to. Though she was dismayed rumors had already spread, she wouldn't let it show.

"Boys will be boys," she said, trying to be dismissive. "Single guys will talk to anybody. I bet he hit up four or five other women besides me."

"Uh-huh," Emma and Michelle said in unison, as they scanned Vee's figure up and down once again, both eyes narrowing.

"I'm sure that sundress pushed him far away," Michelle quipped.

"As soon as you ran off on him, he spent the rest of the day trying to find you. I think he even asked Pastor Flores about you."

Electricity ran across her spine at those words. She took a couple deep, silent breaths and shook it off. Emma was just picking at her, trying to get under her skin.

Right?

It didn't matter.

"I did see him speaking to that new girl, Lois, from the community, though. They even took a selfie together."

A confusing tidal wave of emotions hit Vee at that point. A breeze of relief, a twinge of alarm... was that a stab of jealousy too?

After processing all those emotions and giving herself nano seconds to dwell on each, what she ended up saying was:

"Oh really? Sounds like it's pretty serious between the two of them, then. That's good. But it was Lois I was looking for. Did anyone contact her?"

"I did," Michelle said with a subtle nod. "Gave her a church business card, and she took a pic of that too. Crisis averted."

"Except you didn't even introduce yourself, and barely said hello," Emma said with a chuckle. "You just threw the church card in her hand and left without waiting for a reply. Would it have killed you to at least smile?"

The three women laughed, even though Emma's words were more truth than jest. Also, the mini-lecture wasn't the first time Emma, or Vee, had said something similar. Michelle was more task-oriented than most, and often missed the human touch.

Part of the reason the three worked so well was because of the balance they brought to each other. Viorica fit in by being the bridge between the two personality extremes. She would help Emma dial back when necessary, and help draw Michelle out. The trio was usually unstoppable when it came time to get to work.

More than once, Vee wondered how long it would last. She hoped it would always stay the same, but she knew it was only a matter of time before things drastically changed.

For now, though, there was peace, there was friendship, and there was a purpose. The only thing that mattered was making the most of the opportunity in front of them. They set off together, swarming to finish the breakdown and cleanup for the evening.

After everything had been packed up, Alloise had given the final speech congratulating them all on a successful day. Dishes were washed and dried, the equipment stowed, and everyone walked to their cars together in the golden hour approaching twilight.

Viorica managed to catch a glimpse of Emma and Wendle, holding hands as they lazily sauntered to their sedan. They'd been married for close to two years, and Emma still had a skip in her step, like a little girl, when she held his hand. At their vehicle, they embraced, him gently lifting her off the ground and kissing the top of her head.

Vee smiled a little at the display, sitting in her own vehicle and watching the couple drive off together. A part of her wondered if, in the modern dating realm she was forced to live in, she would know how it felt to be so deeply, and simply, loved.

But mostly, she spent her time trying to convince herself that she didn't care. She twisted the key in the ignition, offered quick praise when the engine turned over, and took off towards home.

Viorica shut the door, not bothering to turn on the lights. The combination of darkness and silence instantly brought her energy down to the point where she could relax enough to sleep.

Maybe.

She removed her shoes and dropped them on the mat with a small sigh of relief. She had been in the battle long enough for today, it was time to unwind.

Three steps brought her into the tiny living room, by the pile of pillows on the floor she used until she could find the couch of her dreams. Three more steps got her past the garage-sale coffee table. A few more steps brought her past the ¾ bathroom and into her bedroom.

"Modest" and "cozy" was the way the apartment staff had described the place. All she had heard was "this was affordable" so she jumped at it. She was barely home anyway, but some days, like today, she missed being able to soak in a hot bath to unwind.

The only way that would happen anytime soon would be to move back in with her parents, in Altamonte Springs.

She would rather go without.

In her room, she quickly changed out of her clothes from the day, tossing them in or close enough to a hamper in the corner. She put on her favorite pair of pajamas, not worrying about brushing her hair or anything else. Today had taken everything; she needed sleep.

She thought about cracking open her window, but then remembered the geckoes were out. She preferred they stayed outside, so instead, she turned her fan on low, lay flat on her back amidst a sea of pillows and blankets, closed her eyes, took a deep breath...

Thoughts, unbidden, immediately raced towards Will. A cool, calm night, like tonight, would usually be spent walking together, gazing at the stars and dreaming.

She turned to her side, as if to dodge the memories. Will was out of her life. Though she was broken at the time, and felt as if she would never regain herself, she had healed. One day, she looked up and realized she was better off without him.

Will made his choice, years ago, and she had made hers. She decided she would place God first in her life, and God was more than enough.

But on nights like tonight, it didn't seem so.

Seeing Emma, her thoughts went there on their own: how could a person so sheltered, so....clueless about the world have a love that real?

Vee clearly remembered, years ago when she first got involved in church, who Sister Emma was; home-schooled, no hobbies, no special skills to speak of even. In youth events, Emma was a wall-dressing, never really getting involved.

Emma had grown and come to life. In the midst of it all, not only was Emma currently threatening the only ministry Vee wanted since coming back, Emma *had somebody*. She was at home right now with her husband, making plans for the future, sharing their hearts and lives, relishing one another.

Meanwhile, Viorica was tossing and turning in a full-size department store bed, alone, desperately trying to stop the memories of her childhood crush from haunting her.

She turned to the other side to force her brain to cooperate. She didn't want to think of Will. She didn't want to think of Emma having it all. She wanted to sleep.

When she realized that wasn't happening, she decided to pray, aloud.

"Father," she began, closing her eyes to shut out the walls that were closing in on her. "Thank you for today, my life, my health, all your blessings. I thank You..."

She paused. Something was wrong; whatever the strange pain was, it wouldn't be handled with a routine prayer.

She opened her heart.

"I don't know what I'm doing wrong, God."

Tears began to fall.

"I know I should keep You first. I know You're more than enough for me. You even give me plenty of things to focus on and keep me busy."

She turned face-up and opened her eyes, focusing beyond the ceiling in her bedroom. "I just can't handle feeling this way anymore. I'm sorry for whatever I've done to put myself here. I know it's my fault, I don't blame Will or anyone else. I just need to hear Your voice on this. I need Your mercy and help."

Finally, she turned to lie flat on her stomach, her face buried into the pillow as if hiding in shame at her words. "I'm so lonely, God. I'm going crazy over here and I don't know how much longer I can live like this."

A restless sleep settled over her. When she opened her eyes again, she knew that some undetermined amount of time must have passed. Even still, the feeling, the dull ache deep in her bones, would be right there to greet her the instant she awoke.

Wiping the last bit of moisture from her face, she lifted a hand and pounded the pillow. Sighing, she forced herself to stop thinking, to close her eyes and keep them closed, no matter what.

Chapter 2

"**S**o, they just threw them folks in jail, not even giving them a trial?"

It never failed to shock Vee how much Shalyn sounded like Alloise. The eleven-year-old was only staying with her great aunt for the summer, yet had already picked up her mannerisms and speech.

"Well, they did have trials...sort of." Vee flipped through pages in the book about Salem, Massachusetts. "Because there weren't any clear rules or laws, they had to rely on opinions. Which is why so many people got in so much trouble and couldn't get out."

"Wow, so even the innocent people couldn't defend themselves."

"That's right."

What didn't faze her, however, was the current conversation. Vee had been tasked by Alloise to help Shalyn get a leg up on her reading curriculum for the next year. Most people would be put off with discussing the Salem Witch Trials with a middle schooler. As it stood, this wasn't even the strangest, or most mature, conversation Vee had ever had with Shalyn since they'd known each other.

"What happened to the people they found guilty?"

"A lot of them were put in jail, but eventually released. A few ended up being executed."

Shalyn's eyes went wide. "I thought these were church people?!"

Vee nodded. "They were. But sometimes church people forget what they're supposed to be doing, and they start acting like everyone else. Except it's worse because they use God, and hide behind the Bible, to make it sound like they're right."

"That's crazy to me," Shalyn said, writing something down on her collection of notes before closing the book. "They should have let God handle it."

"I agree."

"But how did it get that bad? How did they go from following the Bible to getting folks arrested and thrown in jail because they were angry at them?"

"Because the problems, all the anger and hate, were already there long beforehand. Before anybody was accused, they had already stopped living by God's word. The Trials just gave them an excuse to tear each other down more."

Shalyn set aside her notebook, from which she would later produce her book report, and jumped onto the couch next to Vee. "I hope more churches don't turn out like that. How will lost people want what we have if we keep destroying each other?"

The worries that accelerated literature courses would be overwhelming for Shalyn were, so far, unfounded.

Where she had once struggled in school, she was now thriving. There was talk beforehand of putting her in summer courses, since her grades had been poor. But Alloise made the right call by convincing her parents to allow her to test out of a grade.

As it turns out, Shalyn was just bored. Not having anyone to talk to on her level of intellect made going to school a burden. Now, she had a whole new set of peers to look forward to that would challenge her in the fall. Plus, over the summer, she had Alloise, a former teacher, and Vee, a bookworm who knew too little about too many things, to keep her mind engaged.

With the task done, Shalyn pulled her phone out of her pocket and loaded her social media in no time. Alloise stopped her whenever she caught her logging on, so Shalyn capitalized on the free moments she got to endlessly scroll.

She lay her head down on Vee's lap while she flipped through post after post. Vee enjoyed social media, but couldn't keep up with the flood of content Shalyn absorbed on a daily basis.

"What are you watching now?" she asked, getting dizzy from the images whipping by.

"Looking through Sunshine's page," Shalyn said, not looking up. "She's posted a few new ones, but not her usual content. It looks like she went to a festival or something."

Vee shook her head, not bothering to look on. Sunshine, apparently a Florida native, was all the rage lately in Shalyn's life. Instead, Vee focused on planning out her next speech at the Ladies' small group night coming up.

Those nights were crucial, Alloise often reminded her, because it saw the most turnout, apart from Sunday services. It was her biggest chance to connect with the youth on a personal level. Those connections would be key when it came time to move into a leadership role.

Preparations needed to be made, because you never knew what the youth girls would surprise you with...

"Ooh, he's kinda cute," Shalyn said, still scrolling on her phone. "When are you gonna find a boyfriend anywa—"

Vee moved, quick as a cat, to snatch the phone out of Shalyn's hand.

"Ookay, you're done with that," she said.

Without looking at the screen, she quickly shut down the app before handing it back. If Alloise had been there they *both* would have caught the fire.

And she was not going to dignify that follow-up question with a response right now.

"Come on, let's go get ice cream."

Shalyn stopped mid-whine of protest, smiled, and ran to get her shoes.

They pulled up to the roadside ice cream shack in the tourist-trap part of town. Even though Vee had seen everything the neighborhood had to offer, they had the cheapest, and therefore the best, ice cream around.

She procured two heaping cones; mint chocolate chip for herself, strawberry cheesecake for Shalyn. They sat at a bench outside the ice cream shack, under a parasol to ward off the heat for a few precious minutes.

They almost made it without incident, but, just as they finished, Vee felt Shalyn tapping her arm furiously. She looked over, startled.

"Wha—"

"It's that guy," Shalyn said, fully pointing, not bothering to be subtle in the slightest. Vee followed her extended finger and recoiled when she saw Archer, who smiled and made straight for them.

Shalyn was saying something else, but Vee didn't hear it. Vee was frozen, trying to decide if she should make a break for it, or stand her ground and politely send him away. She didn't even have a chance to check and see if she had ice cream on her face.

She hesitated too long, and he was in front of her. Shalyn drifted just behind her, affixing him with a wide-eyed stare.

"Hi Viorica, great to see you!" His deep voice carried well across the short distance as he closed in. There was the goofy smile again, that made her feel just as goofy.

She cleared her throat and took a deep breath. "Yeah...you too." This was not a time to show weakness. If she seemed afraid, he might suddenly get bold enough to ask her on a date, and that was *not* happening today.

"Everyone said this is the best ice cream shop in the city. I didn't think I'd see you here though, seems like I found my new favorite place!"

He grinned, with teeth. It sounded like he was impressed by his own flirtation.

"Yeah, it is. Enjoy it," she said with a chuckle as she put her sunglasses back on.

"Well, if you're here, of course you'll join me. What would you like? It's my treat today."

"Oh, we were leaving. We already had our cones, just finished them." She was speaking way too quickly, and a little too loudly. Her heart was racing, in what felt like panic.

Was it panic, though?

He leaned to see around her. "Who's 'we', exactly?" He smiled at Shalyn.

"Hello young lady, who might you be?"

Shalyn stepped around and extended her hand. "Shalyn," she mumbled, still staring wide-eyed. Archer shook it daintily.

"A pleasure to meet you, Shalyn. My name is Archer."

"Are you famous?" Shalyn asked.

Vee flinched. What on earth?

Archer just laughed as he shook his head. "Oh no, I'm not famous. I'm new in town, getting to know everybody. And, I'm going to start attending the First Pentecostal Church. Is that where you go?"

Vee furiously blushed again. She was going to have to dodge him at church too?

"She's just visiting for the summer," she said, moving Shalyn back behind her. "And sorry, we really need to be going. She has homework to do, and...chores. Yeah, chores."

"That sounds fun," he said, dryly. "I hope you don't have to spend the whole summer doing chores and homework, Shalyn."

From behind Vee's back, Shalyn only shook her head in reply.

"Well, we should be going..."

"Hey, Viorica, quick question?"

She froze in place mid-stride, and found herself focused on him as if he were the only person in the world at that moment.

"I'm going to be at church tomorrow morning, and I want to keep exploring the city. Would you care to meet me for lunch after the service? I hear the food at Soria's is to die for."

She LOVED Soria's. She also couldn't remember the last time she ate there because it was firmly outside her budget.

"I, um...uh. Nope, sorry. I wish I could, but I can't."

She grabbed Shalyn by the arm and nearly dragged her to the car. Archer was trying to say something else, but she wasn't going to give him the chance to talk her down.

Not that he would have had to work hard at it. Those garlic breadsticks were her weakness...

"That was smooth," Shalyn remarked once they were out of earshot.

"Not a word, you."

They got in the car, she cranked the engine with fury, slammed it into gear, and they sped off. She could see Shalyn smirking at her in the passenger seat. Vee knew she wouldn't say anything yet, but she also knew that the jokes were soon to come, and Alloise would have the full story before the day was out.

She was speeding more than usual as she raced back to Alloise's home. At some point she realized she had been holding her breath too, and let out a deep exhale to try and steady her nerves. Why this guy had such an effect on her, she wasn't sure.

Shalyn started to pipe up and say something. Vee decided to cut her off to avoid any more awkwardness.

"Why'd you ask him if he was famous?"

Shalyn had her phone out of her pocket again and went back to scrolling social media.

"Because he was in a post on Sunshine's page."

Viorica didn't think anything of it. She kept her foot on the gas as she raced back.

Chapter 3

The Sunday morning service was electric. Newcomers from the community brought enthusiasm that simply couldn't be matched.

Viorica left the ladies' room, her white floral print dress realigned perfectly with her lace-lined church hat. Her handbag, which held her hair sprays and all the accessories to reset her look, was tucked under her arm as she made her way to the meeting room.

Officially, she was only there to audit the leadership meeting, because for the time, she was a glorified intern. Still, she needed to maintain her image in case they called on her to speak. Young or old, appearance mattered in these things, and even heartfelt worship couldn't be used as an excuse to show up sloppy.

She walked purposefully down the plush-carpeted hall to the sleek, modern conference room. Inside, a polished oak table and black mesh backed office chairs awaited.

More than 12 women were already in the room, including Emma and Michelle in the corner. She sat next to them with a pleasant smile, waiting for Alloise to lead the meeting.

"Did you get a chance to meet any of the first-time visitors?" Emma had a mischievous glean in her eyes. Vee knew she was referring to Archer, who, true to his word, showed up in a tight-fitting power suit. She kept catching fleeting glimpses of him the entire service, and tried to not let it hinder her worship.

It was intriguing, though, that he didn't seem overwhelmed in a Pentecostal church. Most guys who only showed up to church in an effort to impress her were either scared out of their minds when the hair pins started flying, or tried too hard to act cool and looked completely out of place.

He was neither. He was on his feet engaging with the sermon, and even stayed during altar call to pray with a couple people. She would have sworn, during one of the brief moments she couldn't avoid looking his way, that she saw tears on his face while in a slower, more reserved worship moment.

It wasn't a test by any means, but if it were, he might have passed with flying colors. She was curious what his church background was.

But, there was no chance she was going to ask him anytime soon. After altar service, she ended up leaving the sanctuary before he did.

Viorica smirked, and would have said something sassy to Emma in reply, but right then Alloise came into the room like a rushing wind.

"Ok ladies, thank you for meeting. I'll make this quick, I'm sure we all want to get to lunch before the crowds."

Alloise knocked out several points, starting with 'Thank-You's for working the picnic, results of the fund raiser, and then on to how many visitors they had. She smoothly segued to the next event, the summer home Bible study.

"I think we need to start laying the foundation now for our students," she explained. "We have 11 young girls aging into the Ladies' ministry this fall, so we want to get the ones who want to be involved on the path now."

She turned to face the interns in their corner. She gave Vee a slight smile. "Our lovely junior ministry candidates have volunteered to hold small group meetings throughout the summer. The very first one to kick it off will be held this week, Thursday. Sister Emma Hardy has graciously offered to host in her home. Ladies, would you like to explain the event?"

They all stood in unison.

"We're so blessed to be able to serve this ministry," Emma began, formally. "We are sanctified proud, as our pastor would say, of the young ladies joining, and greatly expecting a move of God this week."

The ladies gave solemn nods and a few half-smiles at Emma's rehearsed lines. As she sat down, Vee took a couple small steps forward.

"Amen, sister Emma. We're so thankful to our pastor and first lady for this opportunity. I know it's important that the youth establish a foundation of faith now, and start building their own Godly heritage. That's why we're praying, day and night, for the chance to impart something to them through this ministry, and, should the Lord tarry, we'll see a revival like never before!"

More smiles, more somber church nods. They were killing it.

Vee smiled and stepped elegantly to her seat. Michelle, ever hating to be the center of attention, took a step back and looked down at her feet.

"We're going to have a baked potato bar," she mumbled.

Michelle plopped back down in her chair before the words were fully out.

A few more nods, and a light smattering of applause born of confusion. Vee's face went red as she willed herself not to cackle.

Alloise coughed a couple times to hide her own laughter, and then quickly continued.

"Amen, yes, thank you sisters. We'll all be praying for a blessed time. Now, looking ahead..."

After more short-term goal setting, the meeting ended in record time. The other ladies took off in a hurry; everyone was dashing to get to lunch before the rush. 99% of the efforts would be in vain.

Viorica decided she would head home to avoid the eternal struggle. As she made her way to the side exit that led to the parking lot, she felt a tap on her shoulder. She turned to see Alloise, heading the opposite way.

"Pastor wants a word with you," she said, motioning her towards the main entrance, back towards the sanctuary.

Pastor Samuel Flores was waiting for her by the side exit of the sanctuary. He was a kind man, with a warm spirit. He had been elected as pastor three years ago, and relocated his family from New York to accept the role.

His welcoming demeanor helped him excel at the personal side of the ministry. Even being new to the congregation it felt as if he had always been part of the family.

"Praise the Lord, sister Vee!" he said, greeting her with a smile as she approached.

"Praise the Lord, pastor!" she greeted him in return. "I thought you'd be out to lunch by now?"

"Heading that way, in fact! That's actually what I wanted to talk to you about."

He motioned for them to step out into the warm air. He locked the church door behind himself.

"Have you met that new young man, Archer? He was at the picnic..."

The look on Vee's face must have said it all. He let his words trail off, and gave a smirk.

"Pastor, I don't know what you heard, but I promise—"

Pastor Flores held up a hand, shaking his head.

"No need to explain anything, sister Vee. I was just curious what the dynamic was. He came to me and asked to become a member of the church. But, in the same breath, he also asked if anyone was courting you, at the moment."

Vee's heart skipped a beat.

"He actually used that word, too. 'Courting'. I wanted to know what you thought of him? If you aren't feeling the same, I'll tell him to leave you alone."

"I..."

All at once, Viorica's mind went completely blank. The whiplash of emotions, going from absolutely mortified that pastor was talking to her about this, to thinking that he would shut down Archer once and for all, left her blindsided.

It would be handy, and take so much stress off her shoulders, if Pastor Flores did tell Archer to keep away...

...But at the same time, she knew, with 100% certainty, that she did *not* want him to do that.

She also couldn't explain why not.

"I'm not sure yet," was what she settled on. When Pastor Flores raised his eyebrows and grinned wider, she put her hand to her head.

"No! I mean...I'm not sure if it's that serious yet. I don't know him enough to *like* him. He's...it's strange."

He nodded. "I understand. I don't want to put any pressure on you while you make up your mind. If you need me to tell him to ease up a little, I can do that for you."

"Thank you, pastor." The relief was palpable. Vee felt her back muscles loosen up at just those words.

"I'll tell you what," Pastor continued as he reached his car. "We're keeping our tradition of taking a new church member out to Soria's for lunch today. He'll be there with a crowd, there should be at least ten others. If you want to come along, maybe it'll be a chance to see him in a group setting where you won't feel cornered. We'll even treat you."

There was no way she was going to turn down an invitation to Soria's a *second* time that weekend. Especially if someone other than Archer was buying her meal.

"That sounds like a deal!"

They approached the Flores family's minivan. Pastor's wife, Angelica, was in the front seat, in the AC, waiting for her husband.

Vee greeted her as she climbed into the middle row. They headed off into the sleepy afternoon.

They drove through a blend of vibrant greenery and sleek, modern buildings. They managed to weave their way through the traffic of the burgeoning lunch rush, down the industrial street that took them to the southwest corner of the city where Soria's stood, the premier post-church lunch location.

Vee did her best to contain herself from sprinting to the door the moment they parked. She could smell fresh baked bread being carried out the oven in waves of serving platters. She walked behind the Flores, letting them lead the way to the reserved party room.

Several older saints from the church were already in attendance, including the elders of the Hardy family, Emma's aunts and uncles. And, of course, Archer was right in the middle of them all.

She walked into what seemed him telling his life story. As soon as Vee walked in the room, though, all bets were off. He broke off mid-sentence and smiled, waving her over to an empty seat that was oh-so-conveniently right next to him.

Smiling to everyone at the table, she ignored his gestures and sat at a different vacant spot, three chairs down from him. The choice was strategic: far enough to maintain distance, close enough to be involved in his conversations.

He didn't seem to register her actions as a slight, for which she was grateful. He merely went on with his narrative once everyone was settled.

"That's basically how I ended up here," he said to the table. "The church in Oak Hills, sadly, was starting the process of closing their doors, and I felt it was time to move on. I took a job as a junior financial analyst in Gainesville, and God led me here, to this church."

Viorica noticed him smile as his gaze drifted towards her. She put her head down close to the menu, pretending to study it even though she knew it by heart.

"Have you been baptized in the Name of the Lord?" Esmerelda Hardy, one of the older women in charge of the baptismal team, asked.

Archer turned the smile her way. "Yes ma'am, I have. I received baptism when I was nine years old. Baptized with the Holy Spirit the same day."

The elders nodded approvingly.

"We heard about Oak Hills and the Waters family," Pastor Flores said from down the table. "Such a shame, they were an amazing ministry family. Do you have any word on what ever happened to Pastor Waters?"

"I don't, unfortunately," Archer said, shaking his head. He took a long drink from his glass.

Vee immediately perked up.

Something was off about his reaction to that question. She missed the story before she arrived, and she personally knew nothing about any churches in Oak Hills. But Archer certainly knew more about that situation than he was saying.

Despite her desire to be as invisible as possible during this dinner, she had her mouth opened to begin grilling him on what all he knew.

Right then, a team of servers came in to take food and drink orders. Baskets of the blessed garlic bread sticks were scattered around the tables, and she immediately forgot what she was about to ask.

She forced a limit on herself of one at a time. She cut it into pieces and ate it with her knife and fork, savoring each soft, lingering bite. She made it halfway through the first bread stick before she remembered there was fresh-made butter too. As the conversation picked back up, Vee slid the butter dish in front of herself, coating each piece of bread before savoring it.

Of course, it didn't take long before someone far down the table steered the conversation off a cliff.

"So brother Nolan, are you married yet?"

Vee didn't even bother to look up. She didn't need the eye contact, and she knew what was coming next.

"No sir, the good Lord has not blessed me with a wife, as of yet," Archer said towards the end of the table.

"Well, we'll get you fixed up in a hurry, young man!" The elders chuckled at this.

'3, 2, 1...' Viorica thought to herself.

Then, right on cue:

"As a matter of fact, Sister Viorica, aren't you single?"

Vee put another bread stick on her plate for dissection. "My husband has not found me, as of yet," she said. "But that's ok, I'm working on filling a ministry within church. I couldn't possibly think of getting married right now."

She knew it would go one of two directions, from here. The silence from the elders let her know that she was on the less-than-pleasant path.

After a few more beats of silence, one of the women fired the opening shot:

"I'll just never understand what went wrong with this generation," she began, arresting the attention of everyone at the table. "When I was younger, being married and raising a family was the best way to serve God. I couldn't dream of being in my late 20's and being single! It's like no one values the sanctity of marriage anymore!"

Viorica finished her bread and sat her utensils down. Angelica Flores, who was seated next to her, placed a gentle hand on Viorica's knee.

Just before Viorica launched an observation about the need to be married for help running a farm back in the olden days, Archer spoke up again:

"Well ma'am, it might be true that things are different," he said, as he finished taking another sip of water. "But the problem is, with us nowadays, we have too many distractions keeping us from hearing God's voice. It was definitely a simpler time, in your youth.

"And, not that God's will for our lives has changed very much. It's just the matter of finding where He wants you to serve, then finding a spouse, and raising children who can help serve in that capacity. We're more connected than ever, which means more opportunities to witness and reach out. We have to think on a global scale, while, with all due respect to our elders, you all had the benefit of only being able to reach within your own community."

He gestured to everyone at the table as he spoke.

"There's truth in that," Sister Esmerelda said. "Our young people need our prayers. If they're ever going to overcome the distractions of life and find out what's important, we're going to have to help guide them."

The elders nodded in agreement again. Their rant on the current generation seemed to be completely discarded just as the food began to arrive.

Viorica made sure to stop her jaw from falling open. With a few words, Archer had deftly sidestepped an entire rhetorical minefield.

Angelica patted her knee again. Viorica looked over to see her give a knowing smile. Pastor Flores had the same smile on his face.

Chapter 4

Ringing phones, whirring copy machines, and incessant, heavy clacking of keys on keyboards marked Viorica's time at work during the week. When she wasn't pulling files, or running copies across the building, she was assisting field agents via email, or just doing everything she could to not let mounds of paper overwhelm her.

She liked being on her feet. The hustle kept her in shape, kept her energy high, and made time absolutely soar through the end of her workday. One copy, fax, or email at a time, and the next thing she knew, it was time to go home for the evening.

The insurance agency was the first employer she could find when she moved out of her parents' house. She picked it up to make sure she wasn't draining her savings too quickly. The job didn't pay much, but it covered rent, kept gas flowing into her tiny car, and, every once in a while, let her spend a little money on things the Women's Ministry needed.

This week, the chaos was magnified. Her agency was taking on a new commercial client. Vee was glad that she wasn't on the frontlines, and was only called to address minor tasks, of which there were plenty. Endless emails flowed, and higher-ups were booked in meetings from open to close for the rest of the week.

She was right in the middle of printing out the section of the training manual detailing waiver and estoppel when her manager, Cheryl, approached her.

"Vee, we're doing a company lunch today," Cheryl said.

She pulled a compact mirror out and began fussing with the ends of her pixie cut auburn hair. "How do I look?"

Vee raised an eyebrow. "You look busy," she said. "The power suit is screaming 'don't bother me'. But, why? What's this company lunch for?"

Cheryl smiled as she tucked the mirror away and began brushing lint off her jacket. "We're meeting the new client! A small finance firm is sending a team over for a meet-and-greet."

That didn't answer the question. "Cheryl, you never act like this with any other clients. Why is this one special?"

"It's a startup," she said. "And from what I hear, the office is *filled* with rich, gorgeous young men!"

Viorica sighed. While she wasn't expecting anyone to fall in love with her at first sight, experience had taught her there would be at least one guy who would try to make a move. Hopefully today would be the only day she had to keep to herself.

It was bad enough having to dodge a suitor all weekend at church. At least Archer would have some competition, she mused.

Which reminded her...

"A finance company, you said?"

Cheryl nodded. "Rich, gorgeous men, I said."

"Where's their office?"

"Gainesville!"

Viorica, on reflex, clenched her fists, crumpling the sheet of paper she was holding. Cheryl left to get the conference room ready for lunch.

No way, Vee thought to herself.

It was a different firm, it had to be. Surely, it was a coincidence. Surely, God wouldn't pull something like *that* on her.

'*My God, why have you forsaken me?*' Vee prayed silently.

The new client's welcoming committee arrived at 11:45 sharp. Despite her wishes, Archer was the second one through the door.

She stood with all the office staff who were in at the time, trying to vanish in the crowd. It was no use; the moment he walked through the door, their eyes met.

He wore another of his athletic-cut suits, navy blue, with a matching waistcoat. He wore a cream shirt, a sensible, forest-green tie, and his hair had been freshly styled.

He looked good on Sunday, in church clothes. He looked capable, confident, and mature today.

Viorica immediately turned bright red, and broke out into a light sweat. Worst of all, he grinned and started making a beeline towards her.

She turned away and rushed down the hall towards the ladies' room, expressing her sorrow to God in prayer. This was too much.

She stayed rooted in the bathroom for the next fifteen minutes, wanting enough time to pass so that she could slip into the lunchroom unnoticed. After a quick round of introductions, she would leave, finding a menial task she could pretend was urgent.

Vee spent the last five minutes in the mirror, preening herself to perfection, without stopping to ask herself why.

She quickly marched her way into the spare conference room. Smaller than the other four in the building, it had become the lunchroom thanks to its central location. It was also the only room with multiple entries and exits. Peeking her head through the doorway, she found herself staring at the backs of her coworkers. She slid in and gently let the door close behind her.

As expected, group introductions. The management and senior analysts were giving their speeches about the company being more like family, working hard and playing hard, all the usual lines. Vee sat back, nodding slightly at the key points in case anyone was looking.

Anyone besides *him*.

Finally, the junior analysts were introduced. Archer waited for the other two to finish telling about themselves before he launched his speech:

"My name is Archer, I'm new to the Ocala area," he said with a crowd-pleasing smile. "I'm also a junior analyst for now. In my spare time, I work as a fitness trainer. Looking forward to working with you all."

He waved and sat down. Viorica hated how she was hanging on every word of his, and exhaled deeply as soon as he finished speaking.

Platters containing cold-cut slices, and decanters of various soups were set up on tables just outside the conference room. Slowly, the crowd began to line up for the food, chatting as they went.

Vee had no appetite. She was moving with the crowd, trying to work her way to the exit on the opposite side of the room. She had a clear opening, and almost made it to safety when Cheryl came from behind and grabbed her by the shoulder.

"Vee, there you are! Have you met Archer yet?"

Vee didn't want to turn around. She plastered a polite smile to her face before she did. She also made sure to turn slowly to give herself time to brace for those hypnotizing eyes.

"Hi Archer," she said, simply. She extended her hand, and he shook it daintily.

Him and those darn gentle caresses with both hands. His strong, smooth hands were suddenly irritating. She wished she had her gloves from her church outfit yesterday.

Chery moved to pass by him, in search of her next husband. Archer stepped aside, while he held Vee's hand in both of his a little longer.

"What a surprise, running into you here!" he said.

"Believe me, you're not as surprised as I am," Vee said, dryly. She was furiously looking for an escape, but everywhere she turned they were blocked in.

The smile never left his face. "May I grab you a beverage?"

"I don't want a drink."

"How about a sandwich then?"

"I don't want to eat, either. I'm not hungry."

"That's a shame. Perhaps you want to join me and the other newbies at our table? We could use some expert advice on choosing our coverage options."

"Mmm, perhaps not," Viorica said. She allowed a small smirk to creep across her face. "I'm not licensed to give insurance advice."

He stepped back to the side to stand in front of her again. "That's fine! You can just let me know what kind of coverage you personally have. Then we can look at putting you on my plan if it makes more sense."

Vee scoffed and frowned. "We'd have to be married for me to be on your plan!"

Archer only shrugged and gave her a wink.

Vee gasped before she caught herself. "Hilarious! Listen, I have to get back to work now. Those training manuals are done printing and need to be collated…"

"Oh, of course. Gotta have training manuals. Well, it was great to see you here, sister Vee. A very unexpected blessing. I guess I'll have to wait until Thursday night to see you again?"

She had started to walk away, but turned back to face him.

"What do you mean 'Thursday'? That's the young women's small group night."

"I know. Pastor asked me to work with sister Emma to drop off supplies for you all. So, I guess I'll see you there?"

The torture seemed to never stop.

"Not if I can help it!"

With that, Viorica turned and nearly dashed out of the room, back to the peaceful world of loud copy machines and constant email alerts.

Chapter 5

Viorica never thought she would be in charge of a room full of teenage girls. That was the very situation that she found herself in Thursday night.

Alloise warned her that this time would come. It was all strategic, setting up the interns as the small group leaders for the teen girls. She even had Vee babysit Shalyn to practice.

These young girls were the future of the church, Alloise reminded her time and again. Taking over Women's Ministry would mean being the woman they all looked up to. It was crucial to have the knowledge, and build the rapport, now, so the transition would be smooth.

Vee thought she was up to the challenge. Once the picnic was done, she spent every free minute planning how to make the small group a raging success. She thought it through forwards and backwards, and she felt that she was as prepared as one could ever be.

It turns out, she was still unprepared. Unprepared, for how much noise the girls would make.

And, unprepared for how much food they would eat.

Before she left for work that morning, she had put everything she needed from her own apartment into a box by the door. After speeding home at the end of the day, she changed into her casual clothes, grabbed the supplies, and carried them across the complex to Emma's building.

She went slowly to make sure she stepped around any geckoes that were lingering in the stone courtyard. It was mating season for them, and they could almost get as crazy as humans.

By the time she made it up the stairs carrying the box, her arms burned. She tapped on the door with her foot, and Emma opened right away.

"Oh good, you have the crafts!" Emma ushered her in. Vee stepped into the warm home, where the air was suffused with the scent of spiced apples from a candle, and the gentle aroma of potatoes baking for dinner.

Emma's apartment was slightly bigger than Vee's. Because of their dual-income, Emma and Wendle could afford one of the larger units. Though still tiny, they had much more kitchen and dining space.

Today, however, that extra space was filled. Bags of chips, popcorn, candies, salty and sweet snacks of every kind lay scattered throughout. Vee had nowhere else to put the box of crafts, so she placed it on the couch in the living room.

"Is all this from the church?" Vee asked. Emma was wiping up the few inches of counter space that weren't occupied.

"Most of it, yes."

"They must have dropped it off earlier today," Vee said to herself.

Emma heard her anyway.

"Yes, we *did* have a certain delivery boy with very nice hair and a tight-fitting shirt," she said with a smirk. "He came and went maybe thirty minutes ago. Wendle met him, I think they're going out for burgers while we're here."

"That's adorable," Viorica said, trying to find something to do to occupy her time. She opened the window to the balcony, which faced the courtyard. On the opposite side, Vee could see the landing and front door of her own apartment.

"Are you mad you missed him?" Emma was still smirking, watching her closely. She loved to instigate, Vee remembered.

She wouldn't give her the satisfaction. "Not at all. I'm glad we missed each other."

She realized it wasn't true. Disturbingly, she felt a heart twinge of sadness on learning that she wouldn't get to see him. Emma might have thought so too, but only shook her head as she went back to spot-cleaning.

Just after six, the first of the girls began to arrive. They came in waves, groups of 2 or 3 at a time. As they came bouncing in, each one was greeted with smiles, hugs, and an invitation to help themselves to the snacks.

Slowly, steadily, the food was devoured. Bags and wrappers began to disappear faster and faster as more girls showed up.

The giggles and shrieks of delight steadily picked up as well. Viorica had to speak louder and louder to make herself heard. She would find one of the girls sitting off alone, not engaging, and work on pulling them into the conversation until the light came back on in their eyes and they joined in the merriment again. She was constantly reminding the girls to clean up their wrappers and trash. She was trying to get everything set up for the craft activity before the lesson.

She had no time to focus, and resigned herself to bounce from one task to another as the needs arose.

The first time she had a handful of calm, quiet seconds, she spent it thanking God that this was only twice a month for the summer.

By the time Michelle arrived, the snacks were devoured, and it was time to start crafts. Vee doled out scissors, glue sticks, and stacks of old magazines while Emma quieted the group down and explained the objective as best she could.

They had settled on a sort of collage board, half being devoted to pasting images of what a woman is, based on what they saw on TV, movies, or the internet. The other half was designated space to decorate with what each girl personally thought a woman was, in their own mind.

Vee sat shoulder-to-shoulder with the girls, laughing while helping them paste clippings to the boards. Almost immediately, her fingers became sticky with residual glue, and scraps and trimmings of paper dotted the front of her shirt. She made sure to give direction sparingly, and offer exuberant praise for each girl in eyesight as they filled out their collage.

She was distracted coaching the youth girls, so she absentmindedly assembled a simple board for herself. Her board held small clippings of women in various career fields: office attire, military fatigues, firefighting gear, anything she could get her hands on.

It wasn't until the activity was winding down, and she had a moment to admire her own work, that she saw, in the very center of her collage, she had pasted a photo of a woman in a bridal dress and lace veil. It dominated the board, and extended across both halves.

Viorica flinched. She didn't even realize she had put the bride there, which made it all the more concerning.

While everyone was lining up for the baked potato bar, she quietly ripped the clipping of the bride off the board. Crumpling it into a ball, she tossed it in the trash, underneath one of the empty bags of snacks.

Baked potatoes were devoured just as quickly. Once dinner was done, folding chairs were arranged in a circle in the living room. As many of the girls as possible piled onto the couch, climbing across one another with more laughter and joyful shrieks.

Emma, Michelle, and Vee took their places, spaced around the room, and began working on keeping the nearest girls quiet while one of the others was speaking.

Emma started with observations about what they thought society told them they had to be. Surprisingly, the girls were highly engaged, asking and answering questions with enthusiasm.

Michelle went next, delivering a speech in a deadpan tone about why women in church were different than the women you typically saw online. Vee was a little concerned that the girls were more fidgety and less engaged at this part of the lesson, but she knew it had to be Michelle's delivery that was failing to keep their interest.

Michelle handed the floor off to Vee with a shrug. Viorica then started talking about choices, about choosing to live for God for yourself. She spoke about how to have a personal walk with God that wasn't dictated by a family member or friends, and how to keep that walk even if no one else supported you.

She did her best to not go too deep. She even had to hold back a tear, thinking about the many acrimonious talks with her parents, especially the last one that led to her moving out of their house by the end of that week.

She was lost in the delivery of her message, so she didn't pay attention to how the girls were receiving it. By the time she finished, they were still, and quiet for the first time that night. Vee didn't know if they were chewing on her words or had simply zoned out.

One of the young girls, Beckah, raised a shy hand in the air.

"What do you do if a boy likes you?" she asked, falling into a fit of laughing with her hands to her face. Amid the giggling around the room, Viorica noticed all eyes were on her. Even Michelle and Emma.

'*You run*', is what she thought to say. '*Run* fast. *Run far!*'

Instead, she said: "You just have to make sure you and he want the same thing. But no dating until you're 30!"

She laughed, and the girls all laughed with her.

The evening swiftly came to a close. Because there were no more snacks, the girls' attention spans were dwindling fast. Emma wrapped up the lesson with a few Bible verses, an invitation to bring a friend back in two weeks, then closed out with prayer.

Viorica was all too happy to let Emma bring things to a landing. She hadn't anticipated how much fresh pain would rise to the surface while talking about her parents.

She knew her parents loved her, but she couldn't, for the life of her, understand why they fought her so hard on her decision to attend First Pentecostal Church. Their family's religion was always an after-thought to them, replaced by money, status, and the finer things in life. They attended church maybe half a dozen times per year, and that was a high watermark if someone in the family was sick.

All the same, her choice seemed unbearable to them. Her father at-tempted to put his foot down, saying what she would do under his roof. She called his bluff and moved out the moment she found a place she could afford. She knew they were both too headstrong to be the first to apologize and reach out. She knew her mother would always follow her father's rulings.

She often wondered if her drive to take over Women's Ministry was her way of taking back control in her life. As if it wasn't enough for her to be away from her father, she had to be in charge of something he couldn't touch.

It couldn't be about her. If she was going to be successful in leading a ministry, it had to be because she had the passion for it.

While Emma was praying to end the Bible study, Viorica prayed, as she often did, that her heart would be in the right place. She also prayed that she would be able to forgive her father, and one day they could meet again and have a civil conversation about her faith.

Parents began to show up to collect their girls. Emma decided to keep a few of them around to play games, work more on the collage boards, or to talk about life.

Viorica did a final pass at cleaning up, and then excused herself, citing her need to get ready for work tomorrow. She said her goodbyes, and was out the door and away.

Her ears were still ringing from the sheer volume that evening. She walked out into the breezy night, grateful for a moment of solitude to unwind. She would group message both Emma and Michelle to review what had gone well and what needed to change for the next small group meeting.

That could wait, though. She was too busy enjoying the peace after the storm.

The box of craft supplies was much lighter now. Viorica slowly made her way down and across the courtyard to her own building. She looked to the sky to check for rain. The area lights that flooded the courtyard prevented her from seeing stars, but with the ever-present threat of showers, it hardly made any difference.

Taking a final deep breath, Vee climbed the stairs that led to her unit. She was suddenly much more tired than she thought; the staircase felt like an extra workout after wrangling a roomful of teenagers for two hours.

She had reached her door, and was about to produce the key from her pocket, when she heard footsteps in the courtyard.

She was never sure what made her check, but for some reason, at that moment, she put the box down, turned around, and looked over the balcony.

Archer was there, in the courtyard, smiling up at her.

Chapter 6

V iorica leapt away from the balcony, startled. Then, frowning, she went back to address him.

"What are you doing here?!" She leaned over and tried to project a whisper so he could hear.

Archer shrugged. "Would you believe it if I said, 'coming to see how the small group went'?"

"No!" Vee flinched as her voice was starting to rise to match his. "You need to get out of here!"

If anyone saw this interaction, she would be finished. Her dreams of being in ministry would be brought crashing to the ground. It wouldn't even matter if nothing happened, just word of a scandal was enough to ruin her.

She wouldn't let a guy she barely knew, and told herself she liked even less, put an end to the only thing she wanted in life.

"I'm curious, though! I really want to know what you all talked about, and what happened to all those snacks!"

He knew what he was doing, slowly raising his voice more and more. The longer she sat arguing with him from the courtyard, the more likely it was that they would be discovered.

"Fine! Get up here, I'll tell you all about it, and then you can leave. But you're staying outside!"

Archer grinned. "You've got a deal!"

He came bounding up the stairs, two at a time. At first, Vee was put off by how excited he was. But she found herself smirking, then smiling, the more she watched him.

She hated to admit it, but that excitement made it impossible not to be drawn to him. Most men who approached her tried too hard to be dominant, or aloof, or show that they were sitting on stacks of money. He was the first she could remember that clearly liked her and wasn't afraid to show it. His enthusiasm was contagious, his charm infectious.

She opened her door, kicked the box inside, and then closed it and locked it before he made it up the steps.

He landed in front of her with a hop and a deep exhale. She crossed her arms, trying to suppress the smile on her face.

"So? Tell me everything," he said.

Viorica tilted her head.

"It was good. It had a beginning, a middle, and an end. They ate all the snacks in record time. Goodnight."

"Any baptisms?"

"We scheduled the baptisms for tomorrow. Too many alligators in the creek right now. Goodnight."

"What did you talk about?"

"Making boys wear pink hair bows, taking over the world, girlie things...you know, this could be considered stalking."

He held his hands up, palms out, and took a step back.

"Just wanting to make sure my sister in Christ had a great meeting. I won't show up like this again, unless you invite me."

"I wish you hadn't show up at all."

That wasn't true, and they both knew it. If this were anybody else, she would have been mortified to be in this position. Why, then, was this stranger able to put her mind at such ease?

It had to be his sincerity. Even though he was clearly here to see her, it was like he also cared a great deal about the youth, and how the meeting went.

"Fine," he said with a smile. "If you want me to go, I'll leave."

Vee crossed her arms and raised one eyebrow.

"What are you waiting for, then?" She motioned towards the stairs leading down.

Instead, still grinning at her, he grabbed the railing behind him. In one smooth motion, he brought his knees to his chest and jumped over to stand on the other side.

She gasped as he landed on his tiptoes. There was scarcely three inches of ground to stand on. He watched her start to move toward him in a panic, the annoyance and fear frozen on her face.

"You jerk! Get back over here!" She tried to stop herself from yelling.

He laughed, holding the balcony rail with one arm and leaning back, way farther back than she was comfortable with. She started to move towards him again.

"Archer! I'm serious, knock it off!"

"Knock it off? The 1970's called, they want their phrase back. Besides, I'm leaving like you wanted..."

He let go of the rail. His other arm shot out and grabbed it in its place.

Her heart was thundering.

"Of course," he went on, "it's so heartbreaking, coming all the way here, and leaving with such a cold farewell—"

"You'll warm up real quick if you fall," she said, smirking in spite of her anxiety.

"I'd warm up even faster if you kissed me."

Her breath caught in her lungs, for the second time that night.

The nerve, the sheer audacity of him, to ask something like that.

She paused for longer than she intended while trying to form a suitably-cutting retort. He noticed, and kept right on mocking her.

"Ahh, the lady is speechless, in the face of my peril. Whatever shall I do? There is no hope for me in this cruel world..."

He let go again and switched arms. This time he waited a split second before reaching out, and visibly fell back an inch.

Viorica's skin was starting to bead sweat all over. She couldn't keep watching, but also couldn't look away.

"Guess I should just let go of it all," he said, heavy with melodrama. To punctuate, he leaned forward, let go with both hands at the same time, and windmilled his arms widely.

Viorica couldn't help but let out a scream. She quickly clamped both hands over her mouth.

He chuckled. Holding on again with one hand, he reached out to her with the other.

"I mean it," Archer said with a wide smile, his voice suddenly low and somber. "Just one kiss, and I'll go home. I'll even take the stairs, safely."

Viorica let the moment override her reason. Before she could think her way out of it, she closed the distance between them.

Grabbing him by his shirt, she pulled him in closer. Both of his hands found the rail as she brushed a blazing-fast kiss over his lips. She did it so quickly that neither one could bask in it.

Still, she felt electricity spark from that tiny connection.

Deep down, she craved more. She wanted to hold him there and explore the emotions behind a full kiss. But her logical mind screamed that it was neither the time nor place. She didn't want the fear that came with his theatrics spoiling such a moment. Nor could she handle it if Emma, or any of the ladies from church, saw them.

That thought made her step back and glance over at Emma's apartment window. The light was on, several figures, Emma among them, were standing around, laughing and talking. None seemed to be focused on her at all.

She gave a brief, silent prayer of thanks before turning back to Archer. His face was blushed, and he was sporting that stupid, adorable grin that made her want to grin in return.

"That," he said, "was incredible. The best millisecond of my life so far, no doubt about it."

"That," she shot back, "was a mistake that could have ruined me. Now stop being a moron and get back over here! You promised."

"That I did. I'll be going, and I'll be dreaming—"

His words cut short as something darted through the air. In the twilight, she could barely make out what the object was.

Time froze and adrenaline kicked in as the thing landed on Archer's face, near his eye. Startled, he let go of the balcony rail with both hands, this time clearly not in control.

He started to fall.

Real terror flooded her senses. She didn't think, only moved to him.

His feet left the edge of concrete he had been standing on. He reacted by reaching forward, fingers missing the top of the rail by scant inches that might as well have been miles.

Luckily, the instep of his shoe slid under a gap in the grate. It caught long enough to halt his backward fall.

Throwing himself forward, he grabbed the base of the rail with both hands as his feet dangled out into space. His chest and shoulders met the side of the building with an impact that looked as if it knocked the wind out of him.

Viorica heard a voice shouting, not realizing that it was her own. She reached a hand through the railing, desperate to help him however she could.

He began to pull himself up, hand over hand, until he was clambering over to safety. Where Viorica's eyes were wide with sheer fright, his were narrowed with deadly focus.

She paused for a second to watch, despite herself. Once he had regained control of his body, he moved with muscular grace to get back on solid ground. It was an impressive sight, so much so that her heart continued to hammer until, at last, he tumbled over the edge to the solid floor.

Shaking herself out of her admiration, she saw the bright colors of a gecko perched on him. No doubt it had fallen from the tree above. She flicked the offending pest that nearly cost him his life off his face.

He lay on his back, eyes closed, taking deep, measured breaths. She was at a loss for words to say to him.

He finally opened his eyes and looked around until he found her. She was sure she looked a disheveled mess, but his eyes went wide as if he were staring at the face of an angel. Her face burned red as he held her gaze. Poignant silence filled the space between them.

"I'd say that's worth another kiss, right?" He said at last, throwing a wink that made her flinch.

Jolting, her emotions overwhelmed her. She couldn't help but reach out and slap him, lightly, but a bit more forcefully than she intended, on the shoulder.

"Ow!" He grasped his shoulder, feigning real injury.

"Y-you moron!" She stammered. "Don't you realize you could have died?! Just now, you were about to die!"

She was losing control, imagining what her life would be like had he fallen. She hated every moment of it.

He must have seen those thoughts on display in her features, because he dropped his grin and rolled, coming to a kneeling position in front of her. She raised a hand to hit him again, and he smoothly grabbed her palm in both of his, with a gentle firmness. On autopilot, she let him, while she tried to catch her breath.

"Viorica," he said, his voice deep with contrition, "I'm sorry. You're absolutely right, I was being a fool. I'm so sorry I scared you like that. And, thank you so much, you just saved my life."

She knew she didn't do anything besides swat away an angry gecko. Still, she let him pull her into a hug. She felt the tension in her body evaporate in his embrace. She held on long enough to finally steady her breathing at last.

He pulled away, smiling again, this time more joyful than playful. He met her eyes, and she found herself transfixed.

"I owe you, big time," he whispered. "What can I give you to repay you?"

She broke the spell of his gaze to brush something out of his hair.

Frowning, she studied his face.

"Blood?" She blurted out.

It was his turn to frown at her response.

"It's...blood. on your face. You're bleeding!"

She pointed to where the gecko had latched on, between his left eye and ear.

Startled, he reached up and touched the spot on his face before looking at his fingers.

"Huh, I am. Well it's just a little scratch, no big deal. I'll be alright—"

She was already moving to pull him to his feet.

"Come on, I need to get you cleaned up."

Her tone didn't leave much room for negotiation. He went obediently along.

Across the expanse to another building, a room full of young women watched, stunned, as Viorica unlocked the door to her apartment and pulled the young man inside.

Emma slammed her blinds shut, trying to think how she was going to explain it.

Chapter 7

"**N**ot a word," Viorica demanded. She pulled him by the hand, as quickly as she could, through the tiny apartment.

Archer obediently closed his mouth as they strode past the pile of pillows where the couch should have been.

She flicked the light on to her tiny bathroom and sat him on the closed toilet seat.

"Turn this way," she said, retrieving antibacterial cream, peroxide, and a cotton swab from her medicine cabinet.

He did as ordered, and she sat to work, dousing and swabbing. She massaged peroxide and gel into every tiny scratch, as if his life were on the line. Her fascination with him had changed. Where before she was daydreaming about the future, in that moment, she could only focus on helping him. Her mind emptied of all other thoughts so she could fully focus on the task.

After a long moment of silence, he spoke up: "Give it to me straight, doctor. How long have I got?"

"With this? Not long. We'll probably have to amputate," she joked, not missing a beat.

He chuckled, causing himself to move. She tapped him on the arm to remind him to keep still.

"I sure hope my new insurance covers it," he quipped. Vee would have shaken her head if she wasn't so distracted.

"'Fraid not. This was clearly an act of God. Which isn't covered."

He chuckled again, but kept himself more still. "An act of God, I agree," he said.

There was mirth and faith, in equal measures, in his tone.

He tilted his head towards her to give her a better view as she finished up.

"Pretty sure you can afford the bill anyway, Mister Hot-Shot Finance Guru. You can always take it out of your trust fund."

Archer laughed again, but with a bit more gravity behind the sound.

"My parents did leave me a couple things, but a trust fund wasn't part of the deal, sadly."

Vee froze and immediately began to backpedal.

"Oh, my God, I'm so...I didn't know, your parents—"

He reached out a gentle hand, and placed it on her shoulder. "Hey, it's ok. You're fine, really. You didn't know."

She wiped away the residual dripping peroxide and stuck a bandage to the tiny scratches. She stood and began to replace the medicines, all the while trying to think of a conversation segue.

He provided one for her. "All done? Do I get candy, or a kiss to make it better?"

Clearly not the segue she would have wanted.

"You know, this was a lot for me today. It *is* a lot for me. Having you, a strange man, here, talking about kissing, almost watching you die, chasing a group of teen girls for hours! It's been just one thing after another today. I'd really love it if I could have a little peace to end my night!"

She began to breathe heavy as she felt herself winding up all over again. Her body felt stiff, and she wasn't sure how much more she could take.

That was until Archer reached out to grab her hand. Then, everything else seemed to cease to matter.

"I'm sorry. I have a lot to apologize for tonight, I really put you through it," he said. "I promise, I didn't mean to stress you out or make you nervous. I really did come here just to talk to you and see how it all went. If I could do it all over again, I'd definitely stay away, so you wouldn't have to put up with me."

She squeezed his hand, wanting to draw strength from it. Even with all that went on, pushing her to the edge of her nerves, she thought back to the little moments.

Every little touch. Every time their eyes met. The whisper of a kiss that left her wanting so much more. Even having him here, being so close to him and, the feeling of his warm hand over hers...

She wanted those little moments. She would have lived the same day over and over again, if it meant experiencing those tiny snapshots of joy, especially for the first time.

But, she also knew what this was. She knew this was the most irresponsible thing she had ever done, bringing a man she didn't truly know into her home. She wouldn't have dreamt of being here with literally any other person on the face of the planet, ministry notwithstanding. While there was something about him that made her heart cry out to him, the circumstances weren't right, and she was putting more at risk than was worth it, at the time.

So she pulled her hand away.

"It's ok," she said softly. "I'm glad you're alright." Vee crossed her arms, halfway attempting to hug herself.

"Can I just ask one last favor?" Archer asked, bracing himself to stand up.

She met his eyes again, and felt the warm glow in her chest at the sincerity she saw there.

"What?" she asked, voice softer than before. She had to fight to even get that one word out.

"Would you pray for me?"

Viorica was taken off guard for a handful of seconds. A part of her was expecting him to ask for another kiss.

She knew, despite every logical thought, she would have delivered if he had.

Instead, she placed a hand firmly on his shoulders, pushing him back to his seat, and closed her eyes.

"Lord," she said, drawing her voice from deep in her lungs. "Thank you for saving Archer's life today. He could have died, like a purebred fool, on my balcony. He could have cracked his moron head out on my courtyard. And if he did Lord, I don't even want to think about how much they would have raised my rent!"

He was struggling to keep from laughing aloud. She kept going because she was doing the same.

"Thank you, Jesus, for your mercy to this miserable fool. Thank you for sending extra angels to keep him through his stupidity. Bless his little heart, Jesus."

She paused to let a chuckle out. Her voice raised as she reached out in prayer with full sincerity.

"Lord, truly, thank you for protecting us both today. And, thank you that Archer is a part of the church. May he always feel you near, and let you guide him in his walk. In the Name of Jesus we pray. Amen."

"Amen," he repeated, looking up at her. "Thank you. I mean it, I really need all the prayer I can get."

She nodded. "Yup, I believe that. Now, I really need you to do *me* a favor."

He perked up, and stood to his feet with a grin. "Of course! Anything for you, Vee!"

"I need you to leave," she said with a smile.

Chapter 8

The next day, during her morning break, Vee reached out to Emma and Michelle. They hadn't shared a word with her yet about the event. Usually, Emma, at the very least, would have sent a lengthy 'goodnight' message gushing about how well it all came together.

Vee sent four separate messages over the course of half an hour. Each time, she saw the messages were delivered, and Emma and Michelle both read them, but left no reply.

She silenced her phone and went back to the job. The office was still a flurry of paperwork and meetings as the finance firm Archer worked at was fully brought onboard.

When Friday afternoon came around, Vee had been so exhausted, she realized she also hadn't heard from Sister Jenkins. Alloise should have reached out by now to see how the meeting went, and prep Vee for the next meeting with critique on what her focus should be. That, and Vee would receive a list of tasks to do at the church on Saturday to get ready for the Sunday service.

The silence from everyone in her world was starting to worry her. It was especially stressful because silence meant she had more time and energy to devote to thinking about Archer. She was still torn as to whether she really wanted to do that or not.

She picked up her phone on her first break and called Alloise. No answer.

She hung up and called twice more. No answer, either time.

She wasn't going to let it bother her. If she didn't hear anything back by the end of the day, she would just show up at church tomorrow and ask what she could do to help. Maybe Ma was busy, or resting because of her health. No need to stress about it, she told herself.

On lunch, she called three more times, before finally leaving a voicemail.

Her day was impacted. She spent the rest of the afternoon sneaking glances at her phone, leaving the volume turned up so she could hear any notifications coming through.

Nothing ever came.

Vee finished her tasks while, mentally, she was a million miles away. By the time she left the office, anxiety was actively working against her.

Before she started her car, she dialed the number to the cheap phone Shalyn's parents had given her. Even that rang a dozen times with no response.

The engine cranked, and she took off towards her apartment. She felt the anxiety, for sure, but she was more confused as to what could be going on that would cause everyone to be out of contact at the exact same time.

It took her almost blowing through a stop sign, and a car blaring their horn as she drifted out into the intersection, before she realized enough was enough. She had to let go. She tossed her phone into the backseat and turned the Christian radio station up higher than normal.

Vee had just parked in the apartment complex's lot and shut off the engine when she heard the soft ringtone. She jumped out, yanked open the door to the backseat, and patted around the copious papers and spare clothes until she found the phone.

She didn't even check the caller ID before hammering the green icon. "Hello?!"

"Hi! This is Tyla from Orange Horse Furnishings. Am I speaking to..."

A pause, and a faint rustling of papers.

"Vee?"

Viorica frowned and recoiled at the question. "Um, uh, yes. Yes, this is Vee."

"Hi Vee. I'm the delivery manager at Orange Horse. We're calling to let you know the couch delivery for Archer Nolan is right on schedule. We're less than five minutes away, in fact!"

Vee almost dropped her phone. "Wait, what?! Archer Nolan?? There has to be some sort of mistake!"

More rustling of papers. "Hmm, well, I see an order for a new loveseat for Mr. Archer Nolan, expedited shipping paid for, delivery scheduled for today. The address I have on file..."

Tyla read Vee's address to her. Vee confirmed it.

By this time, she was hustling up the stairs to her unit. She reached the landing and froze.

A gorgeous bouquet of roses, orchids, and daylilies sat by the door in a blue crystal vase. Lace strands, silk ribbons, and stems of baby's breath rounded out the display.

Vee's hand went to her mouth. Tyla was still speaking, confirming details. Vee absently agreed to everything, and stated that she would be ready.

Viorica unlocked her door and brought the vase inside with her. Perched in the midst of the floral arrangement was a smooth white envelope with a hand-written note inside.

Trembling, Vee opened it and read:

A small token of thanks, which should be followed by another.

If you'd like, I would love to meet you for ice cream at your favorite place. I'll be waiting.

~A.N.~

She dropped the envelope with a heavy exhale. She didn't even have time to process, or decide whether or not she would accept the outrageous gifts, before she heard a large truck rumbling its way through the parking lot.

Numbly, Vee cleared away the pile of pillows that had been her sitting place for months.

Stepping out the door, she waved the delivery team toward her.

Within a matter of minutes, a maroon brindle love seat was deposited in her living room. Tyla, a slender brunette with hair cut to her ears, handed Vee a folder containing sales receipt, warranty info, and a sheet of tips for care. She caught Tyla looking her over, studying her, but Vee barely registered what was happening. Whatever Archer's scheme, it had her arrested.

Vee accepted the paperwork and thanked Tyla and her team. After they departed, she lowered herself down onto the plush cushions for the first time.

The love seat felt as if it belonged here all this time. It accented the space well, even the hideous dark brown carpets. Archer had chosen a piece that was absolutely perfect, though he had only been in the apartment once.

Her head was swimming. Never before had she met a guy with the sheer, unbridled audacity as Archer Nolan.

She covered her face in her hands, trying to breathe deep.

Then, she remembered the note in the envelope on the flowers.

With a gleeful, almost manic grin, she got back in her car to head over to the ice cream stand.

As it drew nearer to summer, the temperatures rose, the sunlight became more focused, and the summer winds came and went all the time. The ice cream stand would soon be packed, open to close. He was waiting for her, at one of the outside tables.

Archer's face lit up as she drew near. He looked as if he hadn't seen her less than twenty-four hours ago. He wore navy blue dress pants and a blue dress shirt. His sleeves were unbuttoned and pushed up over his forearms. He seemed to be refraining from rushing over and wrapping her in his chiseled arms, blanketing her with his entire body.

She found herself wishing that he did.

It was, in fact, the only coherent thought in her head. As she exited her vehicle and approached, she realized she had no idea what she was going to say to him.

"You beautiful jerk," was what ended up escaping her lips.

The shrug. The goofy smile. The sheer joy that bubbled up into his metallic blue eyes.

"What can I say?" he asked. "Gotta work up to another kiss. A longer one, this time."

Vee shook her head, and tried to hide a grin of her own. She was losing ground, quickly, in the battle to not fall for this man.

To make matters even worse, he held out his arm towards her.

"Come on, let's get you an ice cream so you can tell me all about your day."

Without a second thought, she stepped within his reach. His arm went around her shoulder as they approached the window together.

She inhaled. She drew in the fragrance he wore, a clean aroma like cinnamon and sandalwood, along with his natural body scent. She melted into him, trying to draw ever closer.

"I noticed you liked mint chocolate chip," he said as they approached the window. "But are you up for trying something different?"

Vee nodded as he looked down his shoulder at her. She was still basking in the moment.

He ordered two cones of mint chocolate, and they stepped to the side to wait for the workers to deliver. It was only then that she realized she had been going along with everything, not even bothering to put up a fight. And, strangest of all, it felt completely natural. The two of them, side-by-side, him taking the lead, her bathing in his proximity, all felt as if it was supposed to be.

Too soon, they were handed their cones through the window. Reluctantly, Vee broke away from his side to grab a seat at one of the tables. He came back and handed one of the chocolate cones to her.

She flinched, as he claimed a seat and took a giant bite out of the ice cream with his front teeth.

"Delicious!" he said, wincing and rubbing a finger along the teeth.

"You really are insane, you know that, right?" Viorica said. She was trying her hardest not to laugh out loud.

"I think I'm so excited to be near you, the silly side just comes out," he said.

She immediately blushed, and wanted to throw a bag over her head in response. Why did she find something like that so charming?

It had to be the simple sincerity behind his words. It was like he knew he was being ridiculous, but was so giddy he couldn't help himself.

She tasted a tiny piece of the mountain of ice cream. Chocolate mint, the best of both worlds, in a smooth finish that didn't make her eat around chocolate chips. It was, in a word, splendid.

She picked at it daintily, trying her best to not get ice cream anywhere out of place. It made for slow progress, while Archer powered through his.

"How did your workday go?" he asked. He was already down to biting the edge of the waffle cone.

Vee shook her head. "It went by fast, at least. I'm still waiting to hear from Emma about the plan for the next meeting."

He nodded, watching her. "I still want to know what you all talked about."

"Maybe one day," she said. The cone had started to melt in the heat, and she was taking rapid maintenance bites to prevent it from spilling over.

"Well, how do you think it went?"

Vee tried to think of how best to describe it. It was exhausting, fulfilling, eye-opening, and heavy, all at the same time. She really felt as if the girls in that room looked up to her, and she had to wonder if she was ready for that kind of responsibility. She had been doing constant inventory of herself over the past several hours, trying to see if she could measure up to the task.

With all that on her mind, the only words she could get out were: "I think it went fine. We'll see how it looks the more we have them."

"And this is only the beginning for you, right? You're working towards taking over the Women's Ministry?"

"I am. Going to be a lot of work, but I've come really far."

"That's good to hear. But what is it about the Women's Ministry that makes it your goal?"

"Men's Ministry has too much competition," she quipped.

He laughed, a deep and musical sound.

"I need to know about *you*, though," she said, steering the conversation back around. "All I know is your name, Oak Hills, a church that isn't there anymore, and your parents are no longer with us."

Vee cringed as the details spilled out of her before they could be vetted. She watched him closely to see if she had upset him. Thankfully, if he was bothered by the conversation, it didn't show in the slightest.

"Then you know most of the story," he said. "But you can't forget the fact that I'm crazy for you."

She gave what she hoped sounded like an exasperated sigh, and turned away from him in her seat.

"It's ok, you don't have to hide your smile!" he said. His hand went to her shoulder and, mildly, tried to turn her back to face him. She obliged, but kept her eyes down, taking smaller bites faster and faster, trying to fight the battle against the dripping ice cream.

Archer stood and went back to the counter. He returned a couple seconds later with a plastic bowl and spoon.

She was completely swept off her feet, she realized, as he took the ice cream cone out of her hand, and she surrendered it without protest. He inverted it into the cup before handing it back to her. She resumed eating, grateful for the spoon that kept things much cleaner.

"How are you liking it?" he asked, as she began to break up the cone and mix it into the ice cream.

"Not gonna say I have a new favorite or anything, but..."

She didn't know how to finish the sentence. The ice cream was perfection.

He held out an arm again, and she stood and sidled up next to him right away. Her body fit perfectly next to his, as if she belonged by his side.

"There's a trail nearby," he said. "Let's take a walk. "I'm an open book. I'll tell you anything you want to know."

Chapter 9

Viorica let Archer lead down the city streets. A couple blocks away stood the new biking trail the city had installed.

As she walked, she fought to keep her head from reclining on his shoulder. They weren't even halfway to the trail before she gave in and let herself rest against him while she finished her ice cream.

She had scraped the last of it from the bottom of her cup by the time they reached the start of the trail. A trash barrel stood outside of a small admin building, and she discarded the leavings of her dessert before they sat out on their path.

"Ok, tell me the life story," she said, nestling in closer to him.

He sighed. "Well, not much to tell. My parents passed away in a house fire when I was very young."

"I'm sorry," Vee whispered. This knowledge felt like a stab to her heart. Even though things were far less than friendly with her own parents, she couldn't fathom the devastation of losing them. It made every day a struggle, wanting to pick up the phone and talk to them again, versus wanting to protect the daily peace she was living in.

"Thank you," he said. "It's been tough, but I'm making it. I was fortunate enough to land in the children's home that I did. After a few years there, I was placed in a family."

"The Nolan family?" Viorica asked. Archer nodded.

"You got it. I stayed with them for a while, actually. It was a decent home, better than what a lot of other kids ended up with, from what I know. The only problem is, I was one of eight children in the home."

Vee did a double-take. "Eight children?!"

Another slow nod. "Yeah, there were a lot of us. The Nolans were great people, they still are, but it felt easy to get lost there. They were usually too busy to really spend time with me."

Viorica placed a soft hand on his shoulder. "I'm sorry," she said. "After all you'd been through, that probably hurt even more."

He placed his hand over hers. "It was a little painful. But I found what I needed. I started going to church out there in my teens. Pastor Waters saw how lonely I was, so he and his wife took it on themselves to be another family to me...and to the other orphans in the area..."

The conversation was leading to something he didn't want to talk about. Vee recognized it right away, but rather than pry, as she normally would have done, she tried to steer to a better story.

"You mentioned that the church isn't there anymore? Do you know what happened?"

"The pastor stepped down," he said. His response was quick, and delivered just as quickly. She clearly needed to steer more to get away from this topic.

"So what brought you here? Just looking for a poor girl to buy couches for?"

His smile returned, and she felt herself relax.

"I had heard of First Pentecostal, and wanted to see it for myself. I decided to move here before I got the job in Gainesville. I think I prefer it that way, though. I like living outside big cities."

She went silent as they turned the bend in the paved path. As the evening drew near and the day's heat began to fade away, they started to come across more bikes and joggers.

"Do you like the couch?" He looked down at her again when he asked. He was excited, but his face also held a shadow of apprehension.

Vee smiled in return. For the first time in what felt like a long time, she had some power and was enjoying the reversal. "Do you even have to ask?"

He chuckled. "I just need to make sure I got a good one. I took a gamble on the color, because I only got to see the room in passing..."

Impulsively, before she could think her way out of it, Vee stood on her toes and kissed him on the cheek.

"It's perfect," she whispered. "Thank you."

It was his turn to blush.

They rounded a second corner of the trail, and were heading back towards the entrance. Viorica looped her hand under his arm, placing her hand on his shoulder as they walked.

"So, go ahead and tell me the bad news," she said with a chuckle. He returned the chuckle with his own, but looked at her, puzzled.

"What bad news?"

"Whatever it is that's going to make this hard. If the other shoe is going to drop, let's just drop it now. Tell me, honestly, whatever is going to be a problem." She held his arm tighter, waiting to see what he would say.

"Well, sorry to disappoint you, but I have nothing here."

She took a deep breath, trying to temper her excitement. She wanted to believe, but wasn't going to let herself be fooled.

"Nothing at all?" she asked, sharpening her tone. "No wives? No crazy girlfriends? Not a member of any cults or secret societies?"

Archer vigorously shook his head. "No, nope, and no. Never been married, no girlfriends or prospects. I'm the same religion as you, and I've never been in trouble with the law."

He turned to her. "What about *you*? Should I be expecting your billionaire kick-boxing champion boyfriend to come out of nowhere and stomp me into the dirt?"

Viorica laughed. "Haven't had a boyfriend in years, and the last one isn't coming back."

"Really? I have no idea how he could stay away from you. What's his name? Does he go to the church?"

"He doesn't, not anymore. That's why we broke up. And his name is Will."

She *hated* talking about Will. She didn't realize he drew this conversation out of her until they were already having it.

"Wow, I'm sorry to hear that. Poor guy walked away from God and the biggest blessing of his life?"

"He walked away from God, for sure," she said, staring off towards a cluster of flowering trees. "Maybe I wasn't right for him. Maybe he's happy wherever he is in life..."

Archer turned to face her, full on. "Don't you dare let his choices get to you." His voice had an edge of seriousness that Vee hadn't heard from him before.

"I mean it, Vee. You are too spectacular to beat yourself up over him. You're doing what's right and living for God. Don't ever feel bad about that."

They had reached the entrance, and were making their way back to the parking lot of the ice cream shack. The bright light of day was slowly giving way to the muted blue tones of twilight. All around them, the streetlights were beginning to shine, signaling approaching night.

"I'll remember that," she said. "So far it hasn't been a problem. He wanted to do his own thing, and that's fine with me. I know where I want to be."

"Good," he said, smiling back at her.

As they got closer to their cars, both slowed their pace against the inevitable departure. Viorica held on as long as she could, until he separated from her and approached the driver side of her car.

"Don't tell me I have to say goodbye," he said, dragging out an exaggerated sigh.

"Sadly, yes, we both do."

He leaned against her car and turned to face her. One of his hands was at her elbow, the other on her shoulder, guiding her gently forward within his reach.

She stood with her feet on the outside of his, leaning in. She wanted to get close, but not *too* close.

They were in public, after all.

"I have to say thank you, again," she said. She was swimming in those steel blue eyes. "You really didn't have to get me that couch, or those flowers, or even that ice cream. It was very sweet, thank you so much."

"No, thank *you*," he said. He ran a hand up and down her arm. "Thank you for everything yesterday. And then meeting me out here, spending this evening with me. It really means a lot."

Somehow, she felt that he was more grateful for her presence than she was for the couch he had bought her. It warmed her heart to see the appreciation in his eyes.

She was silent for a minute, trying to put the feeling into words.

Then, she pulled him in for a kiss.

It was another brief kiss, like the one on the balcony. This time she let it linger a second longer.

The same heat, the same electricity ran through her, from head to toe. She fought herself to stay, to sink in, to savor every last moment of their intimacy.

But, her mind was stronger than her heart, at least for the time. Torturing them both, she pushed away just as quickly as she pulled him in.

"Best moment of my life," he said in a whisper. "Please tell me I can see you again."

"I'll see you Sunday," she said. A smirk grew on her face as she saw his hunger for her. The absolute longing contorted the smile on his face,

"And will I be able to spend time with you after church? Will I have you all to myself?"

He kept a hold of her arms as he spoke. He was self-assured, his grip on her was tight but adoring. She was about to start second-guessing her own decision to leave.

"We'll have to see what Sunday brings," she said as she gently pulled away. He took the hint and let her escape.

"Then I guess I'll be on the edge of my seat until then," he said.

Archer opened the car for her as he stepped to the side. After she had safely climbed in, he shut the door with a wink and a smile.

Turning, he strode off to his own car, leaving her to try and catch her breath before driving away.

Chapter 10

E ven though she barely got any sleep that night, Viorica leapt out of bed, with a burst of energy, at 8 a.m. sharp.

She dwelt for several minutes in the hot shower, humming to herself the entire time. Not even a day of impending chores, cleaning, and church busywork would bring her down today, she thought.

The silence from Alloise, Emma, and Michelle had been forgotten. For a moment, Vee remembered that she still needed to hear from all of them, but she realized that she would just see them at church, either today or tomorrow, and brushed the thought away.

This new connection with Archer was occupying all her thoughts. It started with thinking up questions she would ask about his past. Then, it led into planning where they would go, what they would do the next time they saw each other.

Before long, she was planning their future together, and her excitement was overflowing.

Absently, she finished prep for the day. The longest part was washing and drying her hair. Once she finally finished taming the locks, she blew through her skincare routine, and quickly dressed in an old t-shirt, denim full-length skirt, and her comfortable tennis shoes.

Passing by the couch with a smile, she opened the fridge and grabbed a glass of orange juice to get her day started. She had her keys in hand and was about to dash out the door, when she remembered to pray.

Bowing her head, she quickly gave thanks and asked God to be with her.

She was startled when a warm feeling, like a close hug, wrapped itself around her, even during her rushed prayer.

The sensation made her suddenly pause. In her heart, she asked God where this was coming from. Though she was sincere, it was the same prayer she prayed every morning before she left home. Today, she felt an extra dose of grace applied to her life.

She certainly wasn't going to complain, but something was pulling at her intuition. After giving a few moments of active listening in her prayer, nothing surfaced. She got back on track and took off.

Vee cruised down the streets, still humming to herself, until she made it to the church. She whipped into a parking spot near the door, and jumped out, on a mission even though she didn't have an assignment for the day yet.

The first thing she noticed, as she approached the building, was that there were more cars than normal. Pastor Flores' was here, and she recognized Emma's car as well, among the others. While it wasn't out of place for people to be at the church on a Saturday, it certainly was peculiar.

Ignoring it, she went inside.

Viorica made her way to the Women's Ministry office, just across the hall from the sanctuary. The office was unlocked, with lights on, but no one was there as she cautiously pushed the door open.

She was starting to think something was really wrong. If no one else was here, Alloise should have been. As an after-thought, she checked her phone to make sure she hadn't missed any important messages. Nothing, so far, had come through.

The past few days of silence were starting to chip away at her nerves. She hated that nobody was answering her, and that things seemed to have changed all at once without her being clued in.

But, as she had done so often that week, she pushed the thoughts aside while she focused on work that needed to be done.

Sitting behind a desk, she began taking a look at the stacks of papers that were lingering. Each item she touched, receipt, church memo, or outstanding invoice, was separated and prepared for further review.

The shuffling and organization did its job: she forgot about everything going on, and lost herself in the tasks. By the time all the piles of paper were sorted out, she had been working for two hours straight.

Standing up, Vee stretched and took a couple laps around the small office. She went into the side room that held the minifridge where Alloise kept a supply of soft drinks on hand.

God bless Ma, she thought as she opened a cold can of soda.

She walked back into the main office, ready to tackle more paperwork. She started when she saw Angelica Flores, the pastor's wife. Angelica looked as if she had been waiting for her.

"Oh! Good afternoon Sister Flores!" Vee stood in front of her with a smile.

She received a sorrowful smile in return. "Good afternoon, Viorica. Pastor wants to speak with you. Will you come with me, please?"

Vee's heart thundered a single, enormous beat at those words. Angelica's strong, lilting accent could only soften the edge so much. Right away, she knew something was very, very wrong, but she had no idea what it could be.

Placing her soda can on the desk, she followed Sister Flores out of the office, closing the door behind her. They crossed the hall and into the sanctuary from the side entrance.

Viorica leapt from fright. Pastor Flores was there, standing in the altar area in a polo shirt and khakis. It was the most casually-dressed Vee had ever seen him.

What made her flinch, though, was seeing everyone else. An entire section of the pews was filled with members from the church.

Every head in the sanctuary turned to look at her as she walked in.

"Sister Viorica, good afternoon," Pastor said. He motioned her forward.

Right then, she wanted to be anywhere else in the world but there. She still had no idea what was going on, but she saw enough to grasp the gravity of the situation.

She forced herself to step boldly forward. She took a good look around to see who she knew in the assembled crowd.

Archer was the first face she saw that registered to her. He sat on the very front row, looking both pained and bewildered.

Most of the people she recognized from church, but had either only spoken to in passing, or never spoken to at all. What were they doing there?

When she saw Emma and Michelle, three rows from the front, she began to put details together.

Most of the people were parents of girls who had attended the Thursday night Bible group.

She searched Emma and Michelle's faces for answers. Michelle stared at her with wide-eyed disassociation. Emma refused to meet her face, only looked down at her hands in her lap.

Vee realized, as a cold shiver ran through her, that she was currently living her worst nightmare.

Pastor Flores was still motioning for her to draw closer. Trembling, she approached the front row where Archer sat. Pastor seemed to have a sudden change of mind, and stopped her.

"Sister Vee, do me a favor and please take a seat at one of the other pews," he said quickly, standing in her path. Vee paused in her walk before grabbing a seat in the next row over.

Sister Flores immediately came and took a seat next to her. It helped very little, but it at least made her feel less like a criminal.

Pastor Flores launched right into his speech.

"This is an unfortunate meeting," he said, addressing both sides of the room. "I never wanted to hold a gathering like this, but a serious accusation was raised, and I can't, in good conscience, ignore it. I'm afraid that it affects our young people, and many parents of the church are concerned."

He turned to face Viorica. She could tell he was trying to keep a neutral expression, but she saw the sorrow in his eyes. The same sorrow on Sister Flores' face moments ago in the office.

"Sister Viorica," he said. "Is there anything you'd like to tell us about Thursday night?"

Vee raised her eyebrows. "What do you mean?"

A few angry whispers came from the other side of the room. All the rest of the church members were looking at her, and none had a very comforting gaze. Emma was still examining the floor.

"Sister, please, now is not the time for games," Pastor said. Vee was taken aback by the stern edge in his voice. "I think you know what I'm referring to. From the people you see here, does it give you any idea what this pertains to?"

Vee lost the tenuous hold she had on her own temper.

"No, sir, it does not," she said. "I'm not the one playing games. You *know* what I was doing Thursday night, and if I did anything wrong, I'd like to be accused directly, if you please."

"Very well," Pastor said. "Sister Vee, I've been receiving reports that you and Archer Nolan were behaving inappropriately. While sin is bad enough, and needs to be handled with repentance, we came together today because there are concerns from the families."

Vee's face had gone pale, and she continued to tremble.

Pastor Flores went on. "These parents here are concerned, because their daughters were at the event that night, and they saw you behaving in a way that was unbecoming of a young woman in ministry. Now, I've heard the story from everyone here. I would like to hear your side of things, so we can get down to the truth."

Vee turned in her seat to face her friends. She wiped a hand across her eyes, clearing the tears that were beginning to form. "Emma?" she asked. "Michelle?"

"Sister Vee, please address me right now. I need to hear your side—"

"I need to know what they said!" Vee shouted.

She stood to her feet. "Emma, what did you say to these people? Michelle, what did you tell them?"

"My daughter saw you bring that boy into your apartment!" A woman she didn't know called out from the back row of the pews. She pointed at Archer, a deep scowl on her face.

Pastor tried to stand in the aisle between the two rows, to stop the exchange. "Everyone, settle down! Please, Sister Vee, I need you to speak for yourself."

Her tears kept flowing. She ran a hand across her eyes again. She shook her head.

"With all these people here, you haven't made up your mind already?" she asked him. She kept her eyes on Emma and Michelle, but now neither of the girls would look at her.

"Would anything I say even make a difference?"

"It might," Pastor said, his voice evoking calm. "I'm not in the habit of punishing people without giving them a chance to speak for themselves. If you have anything to say, please, say it now."

"We...Archer and I...' she started. She stammered as she tried to catch her breath.

Archer stood up in his seat. "Pastor, Viorica did nothing wrong! If anyone was out of line, it was me!"

Pastor Flores held his hand up and shook his head. "Thank you, Archer, but you've had your chance to speak. Let Sister Viorica have the floor."

Vee fought to get back control. She hated this weak feeling, being seen like this. Nobody here deserved to see her tears.

"The meeting was over, and I went home for the night," she began again. "Before I got there, I saw Archer had come by. We talked for a little, he was...playing around, when a gecko fell out the tree on him. He almost fell and hurt himself."

She took a deep breath to keep her voice from shaking before she continued. "When I saw that he was alright, I gave him a hug, because I was relieved. I saw that he had been scratched, so I brought him in to clean him up. He left after the cut was cleaned, he was in my apartment for less than fifteen minutes."

Pastor took a soft step towards her. "What happened in the apartment?"

"*Nothing* happened. I cleaned his cut. I prayed for him. He left."

"Sister, it was unwise all around to bring a man you barely know into your apartment," he said. His voice was taking the tone of a lecture. "You had just met him earlier in the week, and to trust him—"

"I trusted him as much as you all trusted him," Vee shot back. "You trusted him enough to have him deliver snacks for the meeting. Emma trusted him enough to let him come to her apartment. Am I only being punished because I'm single and she's not?"

Despite the circumstances, what was angering her the most was the fact that Emma still refused to meet her eyes.

"Was I supposed to leave him on the balcony bleeding?"

"No, sister. But the Bible says to 'not let your good be evil spoken of'. For better or for worse, we in ministry are being watched all the time. I personally don't believe you did anything wrong, but the youth saw it, and didn't know the context, so they were confused.

"I think we can all agree," Pastor continued, turning back towards the audience, "that what the girls saw wasn't what we imagined it to be. This was an innocent case of a sister trying to help a brother in Christ. Unfortunately, it looked improper because those watching didn't understand. Now that we've heard the full story, and both have stated, honestly, that no wrongdoing took place, I believe we can forgive what we assumed. There's no need to bring it up anymore."

Viorica felt an odd sense of relief, even though she remained perturbed that it had gotten this far. She returned to her seat and placed her head in her hands. Angelica gently rubbed her back.

"Also, Sister Viorica, I'm afraid I will have to have you sit down from ministry for the next month."

Her head snapped back up. "Why?!" she demanded.

"Even though you acted out of concern, not only was it unwise, but there is a church code of conduct that we all agree to follow when we serve a ministry here. The church has a standard that anyone who breaks the code are sat down for a minimum of one month."

"If I'm sat down, that means I can't participate in ministry events?" Vee asked. Her voice was starting to quake anew.

"You may, just not as a member of the ministry team," Pastor corrected. "You also aren't able to apply for ministry roles until the disciplinary period is over. Unfortunately, my hands are tied, but the bare minimum I can enforce is a month, so that's what we'll do."

Vee ran both her hands over her face. She sighed as she sat back.

"I don't believe this was all in my best interests," she said to Pastor Flores. "But I'll abide by it. I need to talk to Sister Alloise, if we're done here..."

Pastor had frozen in place. Angelica's hand returned to her shoulder.

Vee looked from the pastor to his wife, to everybody else in the vicinity who seemed they might have a clue.

"What is it?" she finally asked, when no one seemed to explain anything.

Pastor took another couple steps her way. "You haven't been told yet, sister. I'm so sorry. With everything going on, I didn't realize it hadn't been communicated."

"What is it?" Viorica repeated. She had gone pale all over again.

Pastor Flores cleared his throat. "Sister Alloise Jenkins is in the hospital. She was taken by ambulance late Thursday afternoon. We haven't been able to visit yet, it's been limited to only family. But my wife and I are going as soon as we're able."

"You kept this from me?" Vee's voice was hoarse, and she could only manage a croaking whisper. "You kept that from me because you thought I was a sinner? Like I wasn't worthy to see the person who means the most to me in this church?"

"Sister Vee, that is not the case," he said, gesturing with his hands. "Nobody was trying to keep anything from you. I did mean to tell you, but with all this, and the upcoming vote, it slipped my mind. It's Pastor's fault, I pray you'll forgive me for it."

Vee nodded, then flinched as his words struck her.

"Wait, a vote? What vote?"

"Sister Alloise's family let me know that she's too ill to continue serving the Women's Ministry. She needs healing from God, and time to recover. We'll have to vote on her successor this Sunday—"

He froze midsentence, realizing what that meant.

And there it was. Vee at last felt the twist of the knife from the power play she didn't see coming.

"A vote," she said, "that I can't be considered for. Because you just sat me down."

The room went silent.

Vee stood to her feet. The Flores were looking at her, silently pleading. The nameless crowd was staring blankly at her. Archer looked distraught, watching it all play out.

Emma and Michelle still couldn't look at her.

She never knew if she saw, or only imagined, a smile creeping across their faces.

All she knew was that she turned, and her feet began to carry her out the door.

She heard people calling her name. She kept going, eyes fixed firmly off into the distance.

Emma appeared in front of her. At last, she made eye contact, her mouth saying words that weren't registering.

Viorica slowed, but didn't stop or respond. The look on her face must have said it all. Emma quit talking and stepped out of her way.

She made it to her car. It was Archer's turn to appear in front of her. He grabbed her hand and shook his head, also saying words that weren't reaching her thoughts.

He pulled her into a hug, squeezing her tightly. She sat in his embrace for a few seconds, still staring off into space, until she put a hand up to his chest, and, firmly, pushed him back.

She looked into his eyes and stammered while her world was falling apart.

At last, she managed to form words:

"I hate you."

He staggered back, as if she had struck him.

She had no memory of driving, but the next thing she knew, she was parked in her usual space and plodding with heavy footsteps up the stairs to her door.

She sat in the shower for a long time, letting the water run over her, washing the fresh tears that ran down. She shivered in the steaming bathroom, and stayed there until the hot water ran out.

She turned off the shower and wrapped herself in a towel. Taking a hand to the mirror, she briskly wiped away the fog until she could see her own reflection.

Red eyes and a broken countenance stared back at her.

"I hate you, too," she whispered to the reflection.

She got dressed in her pajamas and knelt to try and pray the hurt away.

No words came. She collapsed at the side of her bed, and with heaving sobs, cried herself to sleep on the floor.

Act 2

Chapter 11

Picture this: a winter's night in Florida. A collection of low buildings casting a pale glow out onto the downtown streets. Bars, taverns, and restaurants offering a haven for those wandering in the dark.

In one of those dingy oases sits a young woman, beautiful and broken. She's among the faceless crowd of those searching for salvation at the bottom of a glass, a connection to the faintest trace of light in the dark.

But, it isn't salvation that the young woman is after. She's desperately searching for a distraction, one powerful enough to make her forget her grief and grievances.

She looks down at the ink design on her forearm: a stylized letter 'Z' with leaves and crawling ivy vines. The numbers '13' and '6' trail behind the letter, adorned in a similar style. Sighing, she lifts the tattooed arm off the table to smooth a strand of hair from her face before draining her glass.

That hair, now cropped down to her shoulders and steadily growing, is pulled forward to hide the sorrow in her grey eyes. None of these lost, adrift souls deserve to hear of her pain, no one would really care if she shared it.

If she tried to share, though, they would certainly be there. The men, rich power suits to ostentatious cowboy hats, would come running to put on the act.

They would pretend. They would listen just long enough to make her think they cared. The only thing they truly cared about was using her for the night, and she knew it.

They always told on themselves, too. Either they would be distracted staring at her body, or they would let it slip that there was another woman in their life.

It was hopeless trying to find someone who was genuinely concerned. But, finding someone to pretend for a while? That was easy.

Viorica had learned to live with that. A few moments of make-believe, one after another, were all she needed to get through the night, then the weekend. Best of all, the attention didn't cost her a thing. She would take advantage of the regard as long as it was given, and once they told on themselves, she would move on to the next who thought the same tactic would work.

All she had to do was sit and wait. They came to her, buying drinks (that she retrieved from the bartender herself), flashing smiles, somehow managing to accidentally let their designer watch slip out from under their sleeves. Or, the key fob to their luxury car would strangely tumble out of their pockets for her to see.

Though it never physically cost her anything, life had taken its toll on her mentally. Every shallow conversation, every night wasted in vanity, every empty glass, pushed her further out in the ocean of turmoil she was navigating, where waves of guilt broke over her again and again.

Every day she spent not reaching God in prayer, and instead filling her soul with every other distraction, she drifted further out into that sea of shame.

But the tricky thing about the sea of shame, which kept her adrift in it for so long, was that there was always plenty of company.

He walked through the door of the bar, and right away his sight fell on her. Their eyes met for a split second before she visibly turned aside to process.

Tall? Check. Curly strands of brown hair? Check. Well-dressed? Check. Well-groomed facial hair? Check. He passed the preliminaries.

Predictably, he was making a beeline towards her. She braced herself for another B.S. conversation where some pickup artist tried to take her home.

"Wow, I'm really glad I came here tonight," he said, throwing the first-class smile her way.

Good dental work? Check.

"What are you drinking, gorgeous?"

Vee sighed, and named a drink at random. It was about time to stand and vacate the table anyway.

"You can pay, but I'll get it myself," she said. He swept a hand towards the bar, ushering her forward.

It was always a pleasant surprise when she was wrong. As they sat at the table to talk, Viorica thought this would be yet another empty-headed caveman trying his best to woo her, but she actually found herself engaged in the conversation.

"I gotta admit, the chances of me running into you, on my first stop of the night, feels like I hit the jackpot!"

She scoffed aloud and took a sip of her drink. She continued to inspect him.

Deep voice? Check. Just the right amount of cologne that worked well for him? Check.

Maybe the beverages she had before were helping, but she liked what she was seeing. Most guys completely tanked by this point.

Vee finished the drink he paid for, and walked over to the bar to order a glass of water. She was reaching her cutoff point, and wanted to see this play out a little longer.

She also noticed him watching her walk to and fro. At least he was trying to seem like he wasn't staring.

She came back and started sipping her water.

"Been going too fast?" he asked.

Vee shook her head. "Where were we? You were telling me what you did for a living, hoping your title and/or salary would impress me?"

He chuckled at her. "No, nothing like that. I was telling you, though, how passionate I am about engineering."

"Right. Except that's boring. Choose another conversation topic, please."

"Sure, what do you like to talk about?"

Viorica sat forward. "What's your philosophy on life and death?"

She was watching him closely without being obvious about it. This was the first curveball which, historically, led to a fast strikeout.

"I think anyone who's really living will be so used to death that, when the big one finally comes around, it'll be too familiar." He took a swig from his drink.

Viorica tried not to raise her eyebrows at his answer. "Elaborate."

"It's like this," he said, sitting forward. "You start out as a child, right? Depending on who your family is, and what kind of awful crap happens to you, you die for the first time when your childhood is over.

"Then, you go through the stages, teenager, whatever, and every time you go from one stage to another, you die again. And somewhere, in-between all that, you discover something that you want to hold on to. Like, some piece of yourself you think defines you, and you end up losing it. That's another death. You pick up and reinvent your entire life, and if you get dealt a crappy hand, you might have to do it more than once, so it's like you die each time."

He was animated, talking with broad hand gestures, and she was leaning in while she listened. A little to her dismay, she was hanging on every word.

"So, yeah," he concluded. "If you live enough life, you'll die several times. And once you physically die, you keep dying after that. You die again when nobody remembers your name anymore, and everything you built is lost to time. So, we all just keep dying."

Darn. He knocked it out of the park.

It definitely had to be the alcohol. Not only was she charmed, but she actually agreed with what he was saying. She had felt every moment of death, keenly, all throughout her life. The most recent death still lingered, and left her with memories she spent every waking minute trying to escape from.

"Here's to death," she said, raising her water glass at him. He tapped his drink against hers. "You read that online somewhere, memorized it to pick up girls in a bar?"

He laughed. "Nah, I don't touch the internet, except when I have to at my job. I'm old-school."

"Hmm, that's interesting."

"Maybe," he said, reclining back in his seat. "I'm Maverick, by the way."

Vee made a rude noise. "That's your adult name?"

He laughed again. His laugh wasn't unpleasant, by any means.

Check?

"It really is. It's on my birth certificate and everything. I would give my parents grief for it, if I knew them."

Vee flinched. There it was again, another handsome guy with parent issues.

"What's that mean?" she asked, narrowing her eyes.

Maverick shrugged. "I was left at the hospital after being born. Grew up a ward of the state."

"Sorry to hear that," Vee mumbled. He shrugged and took another drink.

"But, I've been talking about me way too much. Let's talk about you. Such a beautiful woman, I really need to learn more."

Self-aware and socially proficient? Check. She started to wish she had turned down a couple drinks before this guy showed up.

"You don't really care," she said with a shrug.

"You're wrong about that," he said, locking eyes with her. His tone was soft enough that she believed it was sincere. She couldn't let her thoughts show, though.

"Prove it," she said, sitting back in her seat. This was the second curveball, that worked even better.

"How so?"

"Tell me something about myself that you noticed, if you were really paying attention."

Maverick exhaled, and sat forward, resting his elbows on the tabletop. He studied her for a few quick moments, and she was pleasantly surprised that his gaze didn't linger on her body.

"I'm getting..." he folded his hands in front of his face. "The way you flinched at the story about my parents, you have both of yours. And you're used to being the boss, so I'm thinking oldest child?"

"Only child." She smirked. "What else?"

"Single, I'm hoping. No jealous boyfriends lurking?"

Vee only raised an eyebrow. He sat watching her, a tense, silent standoff, until she nodded.

"I'm single. What else?"

"That question you asked about death is your little test to weed out creeps who hit on you at bars."

"Lucky guess. Either that or it was obvious."

"Nah, I knew it. You like attention, but like to be alone, so you try to find ways to push guys away when they've outlived their usefulness. That, and you don't want to have to tell them why you won't be going home with them."

He was spot-on. Perceptive, this one.

"And, I think you do that," he continued, "because this is new to you. You style your hair like you're used to it being longer. That means recent, dramatic haircut. The tattoo on the arm looks brand-new. And you seem like you've only had a couple drinks before I bought you one. That's telling me, you experienced death pretty recently, and now you're trying to reinvent yourself. How am I doing?"

Viorica frowned. There was something special about him. She wasn't expecting to come across someone worth a conversation, but it was starting to feel like Maverick could be more.

It had been just over six months since she and Archer had stopped seeing one another. While there had been guys who vied for her time, she hadn't seriously considered any of them.

Until tonight.

Archer was in the past, and part of the past she didn't want to revisit. Maverick was here, and now, and seemed like he was worthy of her attention.

But, there was still vetting that needed to be done.

"Decent job," she said to him. "I think that wins you the right to take a walk with me."

She drained her glass of water and stood up. With a smile, he was right behind her.

Viorica set designer sunglasses over her face, despite the fact that it was after 9 p.m. The last thing she needed was any of the junior evangelists in the area recognizing her as "that girl that used to be in church". Maverick was waiting at the exit with his stupid smile. She let him hold the door for her as she stepped into the windy January night.

They fell into step side-by-side. She had no idea what she was doing, or where this was leading. Of course he would have expectations, but she was making this up on the go.

Was it smart to flirt with him like this? Was it safe? They barely knew anything about each other.

Underscoring her point, they were two minutes away from the bar and four minutes into the obligatory small talk when he asked:

"So you never did tell me, what's your name, beautiful?"

"Ashlyn," she said deftly. It was smooth enough, confident enough, that he seemed to buy it. She was proud of herself.

"Viorica?!"

She'd know that voice anywhere.

Before she even turned around, she shot a glare at Maverick. She was instinctively reaching up to push him away from her, but he took one look and, reading the moment, gracefully peeled off down a side street as if he were a stranger going his own way.

With a deep breath, she rolled her shoulders and turned to face the one who called out to her.

"Sis...Emma," she said.

Emma stood on her left giving a wide, loving smile, and Viorica returned what she hoped was a reasonable facsimile.

Emma looked like she wanted to go for the Apostolic hug, but decided not to. Instead, she stood a step and a half away, still beaming. "Wow, it's so good to see you! How long has it been?"

"Seems like a long time," Vee said with a nod. She was slowly letting her smile fade, but perhaps it was too soon. She took the shades off, since her cover was so thoroughly blown anyway.

"It really does seem that way. No one's heard from you since..."

"Since I got sat down?"

Emma visibly flinched.

Vee didn't feel guilty about her words, and she decided to let the smile completely drop. There was no need to stand on useless decorum, or to play along with the song-and-dance of a church she wasn't connected with anymore.

Emma seemed hurt. "That was a hard time for all of us, Vee."

Viorica tilted her head, genuinely confused at hearing that.

"Was it? I don't see how, you're head of the ministry now. Seems like the only one who had a hard time was me."

Her pain, which she had been nursing these past several months, was making her way more confrontational than she intended to be. She knew she ought to be subtle, draw it out, play the coy role....

...but she couldn't help it. It was remarkable to her that she restrained herself at all. This conversation could easily be held with volume.

Emma reached out and grabbed Viorica's hand in both of hers. "You know I didn't say anything to get you sat down. Pastor asked what happened, I had to tell him honestly—"

She knew Emma well enough to know that she was being sincere. But that only made the anger burn more steadily.

"Yet you sure aren't shedding tears over how it all turned out for you."

Emma furiously shook her head. "That's not true, I've shed plenty of tears. Most of them were on the first Sunday you didn't show up to church, and then every Sunday after that."

Viorica gently, but purposefully, took her hand away, shaking her head as well. "I'd like to believe you, Emma, but after being stabbed in the back like that, I don't know who to trust from that church anymore."

"Can you trust me when I say I didn't intend to cut you out, or throw you under the bus?"

"Pretty hard to do when you're living my dream. But I guess it's true what they say about the road to hell."

Emma found her hand again, Viorica didn't even see her move for it. "This doesn't need to be what makes you go down that road, Viorica! The last thing God would ever want is for a ministry to put you out of church!"

"You bring up God like He had anything to do with what happened. God knows I did nothing wrong."

Emma froze at that, so Viorica went forward with another argument that constantly replayed in her head whenever it got too quiet.

"A group of people lied, and even your pastor can't tell when a person is innocent, so they turned their backs on me, just in case. Everything I devoted my life to goes up in smoke...next I suppose you're going to tell me that I need to apologize for leaving, and put myself back in the middle of those people, because it's what God wants me to do?"

"I completely agree: what happened to you was wrong, but do you think you're doing any better where you are now?"

Emma barely pointed to her shorter hair, but Viorica still caught it. "Cutting your hair? Wearing clothes to draw all the wrong kinds of attention? Bar hopping?? We used to walk these same streets praying for people and inviting them to church together!"

Emma bringing up the evangelism days made her wistful. She could picture those weekends clearly, the energy they brought to the city as they prayed and passed out flyers. For some reason, she hadn't pulled her hand away yet.

"That was when I still thought that if I worked hard enough, the church would actually let me serve in an area I felt passionate about."

"Vee, did you go to church to have a position, or to serve God?"

Viorica paused. "I used to think that position was *how* I would serve God. He called me to it, and people took it away from me."

"And if I could get you back in church by making you the head of the ministry, I'd sign off on that right now. But you know that your focus has to be Him! You can't let anything, even a ministry, come before Him."

"No worries there," she finally did pull her hand away again, perhaps a little firmer than before. "I'll never be in ministry, and the best that First Pentecostal can offer me is a spot on the pew to keep warm until I die.

"I'd rather find God on my own. Goodnight, Emma."

She turned as both their eyes filled. Emma let her go.

Viorica walked to the end of the block, forcing deep breaths to fight back the tears. She didn't notice Maverick until he appeared next to her. He put a way-too-familiar hand on her shoulder, but it didn't register right away. In that moment, she was glad he did it.

"Friend of yours?" he asked. Vee shook her head.

"I used to think so."

She left it at that, and he did too. They started back down the street, side-by-side.

They made it another couple blocks in silence, then:

"So, *Ashlyn*, what kind of name is Viorica anyway?"

"Shut up."

They passed by another bar. This one was making more of an effort to be a family restaurant.

At first, she would have kept going. But on a whim, she grabbed Maverick's hand, and spun around so fast he stumbled.

"I need another drink," Vee said, pulling him to the heavy oak doors.

Chapter 12

V iorica stood in the doorway, weaving slightly, while he turned on lights. Maverick tossed the contents of his pockets into a tray on the small table by the door.

What kind of guy her age had accent furniture?

He sure wasn't like the guys her age. She watched as he got comfortable, running his fingers through his brown hair.

He was doing it wrong. Messing up the style she liked. She stepped over, put one hand on his chest, and did it for him, showing him how to caress the strands.

"Whoa, um, hey there," he said, his hands on her shoulders. "Why don't you come in, have a seat? I'll pour us a couple drinks."

Yeah, sounded like a good idea.

"Yeah, sounds...like a...good..."

"...idea?" He finished the sentence for her. So helpful. Cute.

She grabbed his head and moved in for a spontaneous kiss.

The next thing she knew, she was being directed to the couch.

What was with this guy? He was strong, that was for sure. He could have picked her up and carried her, almost.

It would have been so hot if he did.

He disappeared, and his voice resonated through the room: "You want a glass of wine? I have a nice red."

What kind of guy her age kept red wine on-hand?

"Yes, please," she heard herself say. She closed her eyes—blinked, really—and he reappeared in front of her, nudging her to take the glass from him.

"Just like magic," she thought to herself.

He chuckled.

Wait, was he reading her mind?

"No magic, just staying prepared," he said.

He was! God, this was so hot!

Smirking, she drained the glass in one go, plowing through the spicy, mellow flavors and adding to the drinks she'd already had.

Setting her glass on the coffee table...

...what kind of guy her age had a coffee table like that...?

...with grace that belied her current state of inebriation, she swung her legs up, across his, and, with a swift sideways spin, sat on his lap, facing him.

He stared, a deer in headlights, not saying anything.

He was cute, even when he had a dumb look on his face.

"I'm sweating. It's hot in here," she said. She moved to pull her shirt over her head and fling it to the floor.

At least, that was the plan. It got stuck somewhere between her bra and her chin.

"Wow...gee whiz, ok. Hang on, I'll help you," he said.

One hand still holding his wine glass, he reached around to gather her hair out of the way.

He then firmly brought her hands down, replacing the shirt on her shoulders.

"Hey!" she started to protest. It must have been the alcohol, because his sudden rejection hurt enough that it brought on tears.

"Listen, you're drunk right now. I think you're gonna regret it if this goes any further." He placed a hand on her arm, just below the shoulder at her bicep.

It felt nice. He was so gentle. And his voice was reassuring, even through the fog in her mind. As much as she inexplicably wanted to cry, she knew he was right.

Sighing, she reversed her movement and crumpled to the couch, this time at his right side. She faced him.

"Yeah. Okay. Fine, whatever. So, what now, then?"

"Let's talk. Tell me more about you. I want to know who that Baptist girl was too."

She rolled her eyes. "Fine, let's talk."

She grabbed the glass of wine he had only sipped from. She drained it like she had her own. "And Emma isn't Baptist."

"What is she, Amish?" he asked, smirking a little.

"Seriously? You've never heard of Apostolics before?"

"Is that what you are?"

She shook her head. "Was. I don't go to church anymore."

"Why not?"

She swirled the empty cup, hoping to summon another mouthful. She needed it if she was going to tell this story.

Was she going to tell it to this stranger?

"Got any more of that red?"

"Fresh out," he said, holding his roguish smirk. "Besides, you're probably half a sip away from puking on my couch."

Now that he mentioned it, he was right. She was starting to hate how he was right all the time. So smug, so in control.

...he reminded her so much of Archer.

"Fine. Let's just say my boyfriend got me in trouble."

He turned full-on to face her. Redness rose from his neck up.

"You told me, repeatedly, that you didn't have a boyfriend. I wouldn't have brought you to my home if you let me know that beforehand! I'm not trying to get involved in any—!"

She put a hand on his knee, patting him on the leg several times. "Hey, hey, hey, hey, relax. It's my ex-boyfriend. Guy I was with at the time."

He didn't relax. He was watching her, barely moving except for a few deep breaths.

Just like that, the calm confidence was gone. He was fighting to get it back, but his entire personality had clearly changed.

While she was currently annoyed, by that and many other points from the evening, had she been any less drunk she would have grilled him then and there for why he nearly flipped out of his skin.

Still, it was nice to know there was a guy who actually cared about stuff like that. So many that she had come across didn't.

He was watching her, still working on rebuilding composure. "So what, you and your guy were being naughty and the church sent you packing?"

She chuckled, despite the pain from the memories. It sounded stupid when he said it like that, but it wasn't entirely wrong. The truth would just take too much time and effort to deliver.

Eventually she realized she was still laughing and stopped long enough to say: "No, they were just...weird about stuff."

"Uh huh. Them being 'weird about stuff' stopped you from going altogether?"

"Yeah. No. I mean, whatever, it was all that, plus how we...how *I* reacted after. I couldn't...couldn't keep going, after things fell apart. And it wasn't fair to Arch...my boyfriend to put all that grief on him."

Maverick wasn't moving. His eyes burned into her, forcing her to look away and swirl the cup some more. "Was that your boyfriend's name? What did you say, Arthur?"

Despite herself she fell into a fit of giggles again. He even joined in, but he kept up that intense stare. She would have been weirded out if she were sober.

"No, Archer," she said. "That was his name. Is his name. Archer."

Maverick went back to not smiling. He was starting to turn red again, but didn't address the issue that was clearly bothering him. Instead, all he said was: "That's an interesting name. Don't hear that very often."

She reclined on the couch. Suddenly, she was in a losing battle trying to keep her eyes open to avoid the spins.

"No, you...don't..." was all she managed to get out. Her head slipped from the back of the couch cushion and planted onto the seat. Within moments the wine had wrestled her to sleep. She curled up in the fetal position and began deep snoring.

Clattering dishes woke her up with a start, but as soon as she opened her eyes, the Florida sunshine rushed in like a freight train. Vee had to squeeze them shut again.

Her eyes throbbed. Her head housed a steady drumbeat. She was never one to forget things, but even she couldn't remember the last time she faced a hangover *this* ferocious.

Whenever it got bad, she would just pull her stash of hangover cures and start working through them.

She reached for where she knew the nightstand would be, and sat up in alarm as her hand flopped through empty air.

It suddenly came back to her why she wasn't in her own bed.

Vee slowly sat upright on the stranger's couch, as the guilt threatened to press her back down, along with her spirits.

Eyes still closed, she took a couple deep, shaky breaths to try and force herself to take inventory of her surroundings.

First: determine if she was hurt at all. Aside from the throbbing in her head, churning stomach, and slight leg cramping from being curled up on a couch, she didn't seem to be in any pain. All her clothes seemed to be on, clinging to clammy skin. Everything seemed part and parcel with a hangover.

Next: determine if she was in danger. She gradually began opening her eyes, a millimeter at a time, letting light in to try and get her eyes to adjust so that opening them wouldn't subject her to more torture.

Eventually, after a long, painful battle, she was able to keep her eyes open and take stock. Her shirt was askew, as if hurriedly put back on after being taken off.

The implication caused her to deeply blush as a new wave pushed her further out to the sea of shame.

But, the shirt was there, just not perfectly fixed. And there was a blanket over her, covering from head to foot. She examined it, noting how well it went with the other furniture.

What kind of guy her age cared this much about interior design?

Speaking of, she heard more clattering in the kitchen. She gasped and gathered the blanket back around herself.

For some reason, she was holding her breath. She let it out and gave a deep inhale, only then noticing the aromas: coffee, and cooking food.

Her host was busy in the kitchen, it seemed.

She began fighting against the tide of guilt, swimming towards the shore, out of the sea of shame. This wasn't how she wanted to behave, but there was no changing the past. She might as well own up to what she had done, and let this guy—whoever he was—know that it wouldn't be happening again.

She marched into the kitchen, still wrapped in the blanket. Her outfit from last night suddenly seemed to offer little covering, emotionally or physically.

He was busy stirring something on the stove. He gave a quick glance over his shoulder as she walked in.

"Good morning. Sleep well?"

She tried to answer, but her dry throat made her cough. "'Morning," she eventually croaked out.

"Yeah. Hey, listen, about last night...I need you to know—"

"Nothing happened," he said, cutting her off.

"...really? Nothing *at all*?" She tugged at her sloppy-hanging blouse underneath the blanket.

"At all," he confirmed. "I was definitely interested in you, when I saw you at that bar, but by the time we made it back here you had had a little too much to drink for my liking. We came in, had a glass of wine...well, *you* had some wine, and then you fell asleep while telling me you don't go to church anymore."

The storm on the sea of shame quelled to a minor tempest.

"Is that right? Well, do you always go out picking up girls at bars if you're so bothered by them being drunk?"

He chuckled a little, turning to face her for the first time that morning. "Nope, in fact, you were the first."

She didn't have a witty response, just stared. Her dry throat worked a little as she processed that.

"It's been a while since...I've been in a relationship," he said, turning back to whatever was on the stove. "I forced myself to go out last night, at least for a while, to stop being a hermit."

She was a jumble of emotions, with a hangover to top it all off.

But was there more to it than he was telling her?

"I'm the first girl you brought home in months, but nothing happened?"

"Like I said, you were too drunk to make a decision like that." He grabbed a handful of some kind of powder from a nearby jar and dropped it into the pan.

"Most guys wouldn't let that stop them. Especially if they've been single for a while."

He turned and gave her the full force of his smile. Her heart skipped a beat.

"Good thing I'm not like most guys. I'm trying to do the right thing."

She took a deep breath and adjusted the blanket, wrapping it tighter around her. "Who says what 'the right thing' is?"

"God, of course," he replied, tilting his head a little as if she'd asked a stupid question.

Her breath caught in her throat. The sea of shame started churning again.

"I, uh, didn't know you believed in God."

"I do. I used to go to church...outside of Orlando."

Vee immediately thought of Oak Hills, the Orlando suburb where Archer grew up. "Tell me about that."

She took a couple small steps closer, very much invested in this new development. She drew close enough to see that he was frying potatoes in the pan.

"Maybe later," he said. "Right about now, I'm pretty sure you need water, and coffee, and food?"

Again, she was conflicted. Part of her wanted nothing more than to hurry home. But, another part wanted to stay and learn who this stranger she met in the bar truly was.

"All of the above would be nice," she reluctantly admitted.

"You definitely don't *have to* stay, but you're welcome to if you'd like. The bathroom's first door down the hall on the right, plenty of clean towels in there too."

"Ok. And if I stay for breakfast, you'll tell me about the church you used to go to?"

"It's a date", he said as he turned to give her a wink.

Smiling, she turned with an exaggerated huff and started down toward the bathroom. The cold tile in the hallway made her step gingerly as she hurried in.

Viorica closed the door before removing the blanket which provided warmth that her evening outfit did not.

She was taken back, again, as she saw tasteful bathroom décor. The rugs matched the shower curtains, which matched the decorative towels.

Was she wrong about what this guy was after? He clearly showed interest at the bar.

She contemplated all this while she went through a quick bathroom routine. By the time she finished washing, she shook it off. There were other things to worry about instead of how in-tune he was with his feminine side.

She stood at the sink, running water over her hands, and froze as she caught a glimpse of herself in the mirror.

She didn't like what she saw staring back at her.

Ever since that day, she had avoided really looking in mirrors. All the anger, all the self-loathing she carried rose to the surface when she looked in her own eyes for too long.

This time, despite herself, she stayed to get a good, long glance.

Her makeup had smeared around her eyes. Her disheveled clothes were showing off more of her body than she intended, even though she had chosen the outfit a bit more than twelve hours ago. Her hair, which she told herself was more manageable when cut, was a mismanaged mess.

None of those physical things were keeping her adrift on the sea of shame, though. It was the pale reflection of who she used to be that kept her unmoored. It was knowing how far she had walked away from God, even though He had been with her in the hurt when everyone else had abandoned her.

She had gone from being filled with His Holy Spirit, with a Godly man who loved her, to drinking herself into oblivion on weekends. Viorica from this time last year wouldn't dream of being a person who went home with strange guys from bars, and failed at one-night stands.

She dabbed away the stray makeup around her eyes. She had to do something, *anything*, to get away from her reflection.

She bowed her head to pray. Moments passed, and a couple sobs escaped before she could get words out.

She had made plenty of poor choices in life, but this was the first that could have gotten her seriously injured or killed. Only because of grace did she find herself in the home of a man who was not only decent and respectful, but also a believer of some kind.

This sequence of events had the fingerprints of God all over it.

Steadying herself with deep breaths, she finished drying away the tears and fresh makeup streaks. Bowing her head again, and closing her eyes, she prayed, two simple words, with all the sincerity her heart could bring to bear.

"Guide me."

Wrapping the blanket around herself again, she went out to the kitchen for breakfast.

Chapter 13

A mug of coffee and a plate with a heaping pile of sliced fried potatoes were waiting for her in the kitchen.

Maverick was sitting at the glass table with his own plate and mug in front of him. As she walked in, he stood and pulled out the chair across from him.

She took the seat, noting the elaborate and well-coordinated place settings.

"You know, you really make a girl nervous, having all this around," Viorica said. She wrapped her hands around the coffee mug.

Maverick frowned at her. "What do you mean?"

"I mean, *this*," Vee said, waving at everything in sight. "All of this! There isn't one straight, single guy on the planet, or at least in the state of Florida, who has interior decorating to this degree. This looks exactly like your wife lives here with you!"

Maverick covered his face while he laughed. His face was turning red, listening to her rant.

"N-no," he said, waving his hands in front of him. "No wife. Just a single, straight man who's learned a thing or two along the way."

Viorica wasn't convinced. "This can't be something you 'just picked up'. Somebody taught you how to decorate a home, and they probably did it intending to live there."

"You're right about one thing: someone did teach me. But, I promise, no one lives here besides me. Like I told you, I've been single for a while."

Vee shook her head, trying to process what he was saying. She took a long sip of the coffee to chase the hangover headache away once and for all.

Maverick was still speaking: "I'll tell you the story, so it'll all make more sense. You will have to accept that I'm not going to tell you details like who or where. Just know that I grew up in—"

Viorica stopped listening when she opened her hands and looked down at the mug she was holding.

A cartoon elephant, with enormous watery eyes, holding a heart-shaped balloon, adorned the side of the mug. A message of love was scrawled in a juvenile font below the creature.

With horror, and indignation, she sat the coffee mug on the table, just shy of slamming it.

She turned it so that the bright graphic was facing Maverick.

"Explain this," she said, glaring at him. "I need to know if I'm in another woman's home."

He rubbed his face. "I knew I should have gotten rid of that," he mumbled. "Look, I told you, there is nobody else."

"Who does this cup belong to, then?!"

He stared at some point behind her, for several seconds. Vee felt anxiety build again. She was almost ready to leave the table, when he spoke up.

"Sorry, I was just...having a real hard time summarizing who she was," Maverick said. He shook his head and placed a hand on his temple. "She's technically an ex, but it really wouldn't work that way."

"Why not?" Viorica demanded. Her apprehension was making it hard to breathe.

"We were never 'officially' together."

"A friend with benefits? Situationship?" she asked with a shrug. "Why would that be such a—"

"Because she was married."

All the tension drained out of Vee as she heard those words.

"O-Oh. I see," she stammered.

Maverick nodded. "Like I said, the story will help it make sense."

Vee picked up the mug and took another sip of her coffee. Then, while he was gathering himself to tell the tale, she picked up her fork and tried the potatoes.

They were glorious. The flavorful oil and the blend of spices were nirvana to her outraged stomach.

She chewed the first bite thoroughly, savoring every note. Then, she began spearing three or four slices at a time as she dug in.

Through it all, Maverick watched her with a small smile. After taking a deep breath, he started the story over.

"Like I said, not gonna bother with 'who', or 'where' right now. But, I aged out of the children's home, and started wandering after I graduated high school. I wound up in a church in my hometown, and there were a couple kids from the same orphanage who landed there too.

"It was home to me. Some of the best years of my life were there, before...everything..."

He ran a hand across his face again, and sighed. "Anyway, someone from the church took a real liking to me, and my friends. I think it might have been a ministry she was passionate about, who knows? She started taking us under her wing, teaching us life skills, how to cook, how to decorate. All of the things we didn't have."

Vee nodded, her mouth full of potatoes. She was nearing the end of her plate, and secretly she hoped there were seconds ready.

"The church helped me through technical school, helped me apply for jobs, landed me an interview with the job I'm at now. And when I was able to move in with a friend of mine, she was right there to help us clean, get organized, and made the place really feel like home."

"What was her name?" Viorica asked softly.

He seemed to debate whether or not he wanted to tell her. In the end he said: "Felicity."

Vee couldn't tell if it was a weight off his shoulders, or if it was opening an old wound. She started to apologize when he slid her his plate of potatoes.

She smiled, and dug into them as well.

"Anyway, one day, I was off work because we had a long holiday weekend. I had gotten my bonus early, so I had some money to spend. I wanted to get nicer things for the apartment, so I called sister...I called Felicity to ask her to meet me at the store to help."

Maverick was staring off at some point beyond her again. She could tell this was getting harder and harder for him to talk about.

"I don't know if it was my gut, or God, but something told me I shouldn't have done that. It's like something told me to stay away that day, out of all days. But I knew Felicity! She was like a sister to me! I never thought..."

He let his words trail off.

"How old were you?" Viorica asked.

"At this point? Just turned twenty-one," he shrugged. "She wasn't much older, only ten years.

"I should have just stayed home, played video games, waited for my friend to get back. But I met her at the store. We spent hours laughing, picking out decorations. It was so much fun. And when she offered to come by and help set it all up, I had another chance to say no."

"Why didn't you?"

"Because even at that point, I never imagined it would go that way. She had been over plenty of times before; she helped us with everything. I guess in hindsight she was only ever there when my friend was too. But she came over, we laughed and talked more, and the next thing I knew, she kissed me."

Vee slid the second empty plate away from her. She couldn't keep the sorrow off her face.

"The kiss was...well, life-changing, in a word. It was all downhill from there. I knew she was married, of course, but it's like I couldn't stop myself. I was so drawn to her. And, I had never...she was..."

Vee didn't need to hear the rest to know what he meant. "It sounds like she was just as much to blame as you," she said. "Probably more than you, actually. From what I'm hearing, she manipulated you."

"Thanks," he said, sighing and shaking his head. "I mean, maybe. Who knows? Everyone sure treated me like I was the most to blame." He forced himself to laugh, with his face flushed. Vee saw tears forming in his eyes, and suddenly found herself holding back her own.

"How long did you...see her?"

"Not long. We snuck to see each other in secret over three months, I guess? I think her husband knew that something was wrong. One day, she just ended it, and that weekend, she and her husband didn't show up for church."

"Did she tell anyone?"

"She told *everyone*."

Vee recognized that pain, the rough edge in his voice, as he described what happened next.

"An interim pastor was set up. He called me in and told me, frankly, he knew. I tried to explain myself, but there was no explanation. There was no way I could justify, or even defend myself, to the church. Every single person there knew what I had done. Everyone avoided me like the plague."

If the table were smaller, Vee would have reached across to squeeze his hand. She imagined being in his shoes, having the whole church glaring down at you. She couldn't compare her experience, but she certainly could sympathize.

"The worst moment of all was when my friend confronted me about it. Like me, he loved the church, and it felt like the family he never had. When he found out that I was the reason things were falling apart, he yelled, shoved me, told me he never wanted to see me again. I lost my best friend, my church, and the first person who I thought loved me, all in one weekend."

"What did you do then?" Viorica whispered.

"I died," Maverick said. He took a long drink from his coffee, which had grown cold.

"I packed up the apartment, paid the rest of the lease with my savings, did a little research, and drifted around before I moved out here, to Ocala. I thought about Orlando, or Gainesville, but I wanted to live outside a big city. It's better this way."

Vee shook her head at how much he reminded her of Archer. The two could have been brothers, it seemed.

Reclining in her kitchen chair, she picked up her own coffee and finished it.

"I'm so sorry to hear that," she said. "Through all that, you still kept your belief in God?"

"Can't say I really had a choice," Maverick said with a smile. "God wasn't the one who messed up my life; I did that. I needed Him to forgive me, it's not like I could afford to pretend He wasn't still there."

"That's deep," she said. She sat forward again. "Now, what aren't you telling me?"

"Lots," Maverick confessed. She was taken aback by his candor. "Maybe one day you'll earn the full story. I don't tell it very often, as I'm sure you can understand."

Viorica digested his words while she finished her coffee. With the incomplete version she had heard, there were questions she wanted to ask. She decided to save them until he chose to fill in more details.

Just when she had been feeling close to normal, his story broke her heart all over again.

Worse, it reopened her own wounds.

"So, what's your verdict?" Maverick asked. "Am I too much of a scoundrel for you to be around? Afraid I'll corrupt your innocent soul?"

He was facetious, almost sneering, but she knew why he was asking, at that moment. He had been vulnerable to her, and was desperate for reassurance.

"I don't have a verdict," she said plainly. "You did what you did, but you learned from it. And, you kept your faith in God through all of that. I don't have a heaven or a hell to put you in. All I can do is accept you for who you are, where you are right now."

There was no missing the real, genuine smile that crept up on his face. He tried to distract from it, and the tears, by gathering the dishes and taking them over to the sink.

Vee heard him sigh aloud, as he washed the remnants and placed the dishes in the dishwasher. She allowed him a moment to regain his composure.

When he finally came back over to the table, he asked: "What happens now?"

"Now, I go home, shower, and get myself put back together," she said. "Then, we go out to dinner tonight, and try this whole date thing again."

Chapter 14

God's grace continued to abound, Viorica realized, as Maverick dropped her off at the bar's parking lot and her car was still there.

Nothing broken, gas not siphoned, no tickets on the windshield. His mercy was, indeed, new every morning.

She thanked Maverick, and before she drove off, left her phone number on a scrap of paper, along with instructions to message her at 7.

She shut her apartment door and exhaled. She felt safe in her home again, after the whirlwind adventure that was last night.

As she did, she walked by the love seat, not wanting to touch it. She crawled into her bed and stared at the ceiling.

How did she feel about Maverick? She asked herself that question over and over.

He was charming, no denying that. His past was a bit of an obstacle, though. She didn't think the same situation would come up again, but it seemed like he had a lot of baggage he was dealing with. She wasn't sure it was safe to be with someone who had had an affair—

She threw her head back into the pillow. No, that was the old way of thinking. It was church culture that made her follow that logic trail. What had happened was in the past. It was wrong, but it's not like he was still out chasing married women.

Knowing how the church had treated her, when it *looked* like she did wrong, Viorica could only imagine how Maverick had felt, and was still feeling, when something that church people considered to be nigh-unforgiveable was out for all the world to see.

She wasn't going to be part of that problem anymore. Maybe she didn't know how she really felt about him, but she wasn't going to let his past mistake be the deciding factor. She could give him a fair shot.

Even though he wasn't Archer. Something about being in Maverick's presence, while exciting, didn't yet elicit that flare she was missing.

Vee briefly considered picking up the phone and calling Archer. She owed it to him to let him know how foolish it was for her to take her frustrations out on him.

While Archer did contribute to the problem, it was the church who caused the grievance, not him. And, for him to be such an important part of her life, she was never happy about the way she had let her grief come between them.

What to do?

She lied, staring at the ceiling, trying to decide what the next best move would be. She stayed rooted in place until her headache began creeping its way back to her.

Finally having access to her emergency stash again, Vee opened a warm water bottle, drank half as she popped two pills to stop the pressure in its tracks, and then closed her eyes.

Hours passed, and she was awoken by her ringing phone. Opening heavy eyelids, she pulled it up to see a text from an unsaved number.

Maverick, she realized, reading the message. He wanted to know her favorite places to eat dinner. Dressage was in town that weekend, so most restaurants were going to be packed, but he claimed to know a few secret spots.

She instructed him to surprise her. A couple minutes later, he texted a map link to a place she'd never heard of, telling her to meet him at 8:30.

Vee clambered out of bed and got herself ready for the night. She decided a more sensible outfit was in order. The calf-length sundress with ruffled sleeves won the pick.

Showering and hair styling were both familiar, but applying makeup was still new to her. It took her a while to get through all the steps.

Once finished, she jumped in the car, heading for the restaurant she'd just discovered.

She pulled up to the adobe building at quarter to nine. Maverick was reclining on his car, waiting. He broke into a smile as he saw her.

The parking lot was somewhat filled, but plenty of spaces were scattered nearby. She pulled into one next to him.

"Glad you could make it," he said, opening the door and helping her out of the vehicle.

"Sorry I'm late," she said. "Still trying to get used to my makeup routine."

"Oh yeah? Another big life change, huh?" He held onto her hand as she shut the car door, and they walked into the restaurant together.

Low lights and smoky aromas from the kitchen were Vee's first impression. There was a symphony of various dishes, but she couldn't place the cuisine.

"What kind of place is this?" she asked, scanning the building for clues.

"It's a fusion restaurant. Southwest American with Korean barbecue."

Vee never would have guessed that from the sleek, minimalist interior. Nor did the restaurant's name, 'Cravings', give much of a hint.

They were seated right away. Viorica let Maverick order for her, since she was in over her head at the menu choices. He got a spare rib burrito for himself, and a kimchi rice bowl for her.

"You never did tell me your story," Maverick said once the orders were in.

"You sure? I seem to remember something about that."

"You told me you had a boyfriend. Archie?"

"Archer."

"Right. And you got kicked out of church because they were weird about some stuff. Then you fell asleep mid-sentence."

"Yeah, that was the long and short of it."

"Definitely more 'short' than long."

Vee shrugged and reached with her chopsticks to pick up a piece of steamed broccoli from the appetizer platter.

"Not much to tell. My church—." She winced. "The church I used to go to had rules about who can be in ministry. I was passionate about the Women's Ministry, which coordinated volunteers and held big events. I was working under a lady named Alloise, the head of the ministry who was stepping down due to health concerns. She wanted me to take over, but I had to work towards it.

"This guy, Archer, starts coming around and flirting with me. At first I'm ok, because I can ignore him. But one day, he shows up to my apartment and people see it. Next thing you know, I'm being labeled a sinner and heathen."

"But, you didn't do anything? He was there and you guys didn't make out or whatever?"

Vee noticed that Maverick was suddenly more interested in this story than he was letting on. He seemed cool and collected from the outside, but something felt off about the questions he was asking.

She continued to watch him while she doled out information.

"Nope, nothing. It was all innocent. In fact, I think I did a good thing by helping him."

"How so?"

She rolled her eyes, reliving the frustration. "He was goofing around, hanging off the edge of the balcony, pretending to fall back."

Maverick chuckled, but didn't say anything. His face was expressionless.

"While he was at it, a gecko attacked him from the trees. The idiot almost *did* fall. He managed to save himself from splattering on the ground, and I brought him inside to patch him up."

She sighed and picked up more steamed broccoli. "I don't know who actually said what. They told me that some of the youth, who were at another apartment that night, saw me bring him in. I think one, or both, of the girls who were also in the running to lead the ministry, saw it and ratted me out without knowing the story. Either way, I got sat down for it, and the next day they held the vote for who was going to lead the ministry."

"That's playing dirty. I'm so sorry to hear that."

"Yeah, thanks. It was...hard."

The conversation paused as their entrees were delivered to the table. Then, after the server left:

"Because of what he did, you broke things off with Archie?"

Viorica raised an eyebrow.

"I mean, Archer. Your boyfriend," Maverick said, holding up a hand as he corrected himself.

"Not really. We had literally just started dating. It was new, and I tried to make it work, but there was too much I was dealing with at the time."

"Did you love him?"

Viorica abandoned chopsticks in favor of a fork. She cautiously started picking at her bowl. "I liked him a lot, but after all that, I just didn't have it in me to keep going. It probably would have turned into love, or something more."

Maverick nodded as he kept working through his own food. They ate in silence for a while, until he looked up, a puzzled look drawn over his face.

"What ever happened to that lady who was training you? What did she say about all that?"

Viorica put her fork down.

"I haven't spoken to her," she whispered.

She was back out on the sea of shame.

They left Cravings shortly after the meal. Vee found herself sated but not stuffed.

She was also wide awake, and ready to take on the night. When she mentioned this to Maverick, he told her to follow him to a place.

He led them across town, to the east side of the city. They pulled up to a line of connected buildings, one of them sporting a green awning beneath a neon sign that read 'The Boulevard'.

Inside was a well-lit interior that to hosted a live music stage, bar, and restaurant on the ground floor, and several rows of arcade cabinets and pinball machines on the top level. A crowd was gathering, but it wasn't terribly loud yet.

Maverick held her hand and led her upstairs. Dropping both their coats at a table, he rolled up his sleeves and steered them to a pinball machine.

They took turns competing for the highest score. Viorica's competitive side immediately flared, and the trash-talk began to flow more and more freely with every turn. When her last ball zipped past the flippers and her run ended, leaving Maverick as the victor, she laughed aloud, and even congratulated him. Grinning, he motioned for a high-five, which she delivered.

He offered to buy her a drink, and she agreed, requesting one of the unique cocktails written on the chalk menu. He made his way downstairs to place the order.

Vee claimed a seat at their table and pulled out her phone while waiting. She inadvertently opened the folder for text messages, and her eyes fell on the message thread with Archer.

She read through the final, bitter exchanges. Her eyes drifted to the date stamp: September.

They were sent long after she had stopped attending church. The day of the vote, she made a real effort to show up. But as the weeks went on, the stares, the subtle nods to the situation from the pulpit during the sermons, even the altar services where women would rush to surround her and pray, were all too much to handle.

While she loved the prayers, she would have much preferred apologies and honest conversations. None of that seemed to be forthcoming, however. In total, she made it four weeks before she stopped attending.

Archer lasted longer. As far as she knew, he was still there. But their relationship couldn't endure, and she felt it wasn't fair to make him live through the turbulence with her.

She wished she could have found words to express that without making him the villain, or letting her hurt steer them. Archer deserved better, whether it was with her or not...

"Hi, excuse me? Don't I know you from somewhere?"

Viorica's head snapped up. A pretty young woman, who seemed to have Chinese ancestry, was standing across the table from her, sporting a nervous smile.

Vee knew they had met before. The young woman had a round, pleasant face, and her hair cut to around her ears.

"You look really familiar," Vee admitted. "I can't place where, though. I'm Vee."

"Oooh, you're Viorica?! I met you at First Pentecostal Church, right?"

Vee tried to stop her face from falling. She let out a quick breath.

"Yup, I'm Viorica. You probably did see me there."

"Ok, awesome! I'm Lois!"

The lively young woman extended a hand in front of a dazzling smile. She looked as if she practiced her smile a lot. Vee didn't know why, as she still struggled to place the face with the name.

"Hi Lois! I'm sorry to admit, but I don't really remember seeing you at First Pentecostal..."

Lois waved a hand. "Oh, don't worry, it was a while ago. I showed up during the—"

"Women's Picnic!" Viorica interjected. "Of course! I remember that now! Want to join me?"

Lois pulled out a chair and sat at the table. "I'm glad you remember! It's been about three months since the last time I was there. Have you been around?"

"Here and there," Vee said. "I don't really go to that church anymore."

"Oh ok! I heard your name mentioned, whenever I went."

Vee flinched, immediately assuming the worst and going on the defensive. "Oh? That's strange. When did they mention me?"

"Your name was on that big board of people they were praying for."

Vee wasn't entirely settled on how that knowledge made her feel. She decided to change the subject and process all of that later.

"So, it's only been three months since you were there last? How was it?"

Lois shrugged and rolled her shoulders back. "It's...ok. Don't get me wrong, the service is nice. But, it feels like there isn't a lot there for young people, around our age."

Vee almost dropped her phone. "What about the Women's Ministry? I know they always do stuff to reach out to college-aged groups."

"Yeah...they don't do a lot of that anymore. The two who are leading it, Emma and...?"

"Michelle?" Vee added for her.

"Yeah, that's her! Emma and Michelle don't seem to be focused on building from the community."

Vee could only shake her head. Ma's worse fear had come true.

"In fact," Lois went on, "I had ideas I tried to bring up. I had a few contacts that were looking for churches to host programs for college-aged young people. I tried to get them onboard, but they seemed to be dragging their feet, and things move fast."

"That's unreal," Vee said, half to herself.

Just then, Maverick came back up the stairs, drinks in hand. He did a double-take as he saw the woman seated at the table across from Vee.

"Lois?!" He put the drinks down and wrapped her up in a hug, almost lifting her off the ground.

"It's been too long, Maverick!" Lois said, grinning at him.

"Way too long! How've you been?"

"Oh, about the same. Staying busy with all the irons I have in the fire…do you know Viorica?"

"Not as well as I would like," Maverick said, smirking.

Vee rolled her eyes.

"We're here together. You should join us!"

Lois stayed for the better part of an hour. She was an open book, in this setting. From what Vee could remember, Lois had been relatively quiet at the picnic.

But, of course, she probably only thought that because she had been distracted with Archer back then.

By the time Lois was ready to say good-bye, Vee was ready to call it a night as well. Lois grabbed her phone and held it up to take a selfie to commemorate the evening.

The moment she raised her phone, Maverick slid to the side, out of the frame. Puzzled, Vee posed for the selfie, sneaking a glance at him while Lois snapped multiple shots. Once she was satisfied, they all walked out together into the chilly evening air.

"You gotta come by my new place," Lois was saying to Maverick. "I'm doing another karaoke night soon."

"Those were always a blast! Can I bring a date with me?" Maverick asked as he put his arm around Vee's shoulder.

"You better!" Lois said with a wink.

They saw Lois safely to her vehicle: a red electric sedan with a bumper sticker that read: '#Sunshine'. After she took off, the pair walked together.

Vee kept her head down, frantically trying to feel if she was making the right decision.

She believed she had her mind made up. She would text Archer, at least one more time. She would offer an apology, way overdue, and let him know, again, that he deserved the best, or at least better than she had been able to give...

...and then, she would start something new with Maverick.

They arrived at their cars, parked side-by-side.

"So, where's the party headed for the rest of tonight?" Maverick asked.

Vee smirked. "Right here's fine with me," she said.

He looked confused, until she grabbed him by his waist and pulled him in for a kiss.

He didn't fight her. He followed her lead, and drew in to her, drawn like a magnet.

She reached up and draped her arms around his shoulders as her lips closed over his. Static, and tension that had existed since the first moment they met, came alive in the space between them.

He was such an interesting contradiction. He was confident, strong, assertive in life. But his kisses were gentle, almost timid in a way. He had some experience, but even she had more, and it showed. He let her direct when they separated and came back together.

And the more she led them in the soft, intimate dance, the more she realized it wasn't right.

There was heat present; his body warmth, and the heat from the sheer act of kissing. But there was no depth to the heat she felt. With Will, there had been layers of attraction. With Archer, there had been fireworks, and a spark inside her.

With Maverick, it felt like routine. It felt like the act of kissing was devoid of the passion and life that made it unforgettable. Whatever connection fed into it, they hadn't built yet.

It was even more jarring when Maverick suddenly broke away. He took a step back, holding her at arms' length.

"I'm...wow, I'm sorry," he said. He touched his bottom lip, and half-closed his eyes. "That was...that was amazing. But I shouldn't be doing that. Any of this, really."

"What do you mean?" Vee asked, frowning. She was more confused than hurt. Even though she wasn't feeling the passion of their kiss, it still felt like rejection.

He had backed up several more steps, and began pacing. "I just...there's a lot going on. I can't really talk about it." He shook his head as he continued to pace.

"What on earth are you going on about?" Vee crossed her arms over herself. The sudden withdrawal of his body heat made the cold night air that much more discernible.

Maverick looked at her sadly. She could tell he wanted to say something, but was refraining.

"I...just can't," he said simply. "I have a lot that I need to unpack. I'm sorry Viorica. Goodnight."

He got in his car, and she followed suit to her own. As his engine turned over, he gave her a final sad smile, a small wave, and left for the evening.

Chapter 15

Viorica spent the rest of the night wondering what it all meant. Everything, from Maverick's strange departure, to the emotional void in the kiss they shared, made her rethink all of her decisions. As it stood, she was right back at square one, needing to decide what to do.

She made it home, changed, and crawled into bed, furiously replaying the night in her mind.

She thought she was settled on this issue. She began to realize that it was far from closed.

The morning came, and she woke up at 7 a.m. sharp, as her habit had been for so long. The still-waking part of her brain told her to begin getting ready for church, until her conscious mind came online and reminded her that it didn't work that way anymore.

It was useless to try and fall back asleep. She got up, washed, and made a small breakfast. While she ate, she went back to debating what she was going to do.

No answers were forthcoming about her current relationship dilemma. Instead, she began to reflect over the past couple days.

The weekend had been a blur. It seemed like another lifetime ago she had first met Maverick in that bar. Getting to truly know him, beneath the manicured exterior he presented, had been eye-opening. The story of his past had been shocking, and she still hadn't processed it all.

She thought how he must have felt, to be dragged into the hotseat for the entire church to voice their opinion about you. How it must have been impossible to feel grace, because everyone around wrote you off for your mistake.

Before that day in the late spring, she had felt nothing but warmth and appreciation from Pastor Flores. That same warmth made the entire situation so much more devastating, because she never saw the knife coming for her back. She wondered if it would have been easier on Maverick, getting the consternation of an interim pastor, instead of a man whom...

Viorica slowly lifted her head, as a major question arose.

Interim pastor.

They had to bring in an interim pastor, right after everything came to light. Did that mean...?

No way.

She suddenly needed answers, and wasn't afraid to go get them. She hurriedly threw on the first casual outfit that seemed presentable and dashed out the door.

She vaguely remembered the way back to Maverick's townhouse. She had to drive to the bar and retrace her steps from there.

Once she found her way back to the community, she drove around until she spotted a unit that looked to be the same. She hesitated, as there was a different car in the driveway. The red sedan seemed awfully familiar.

Vee idled in the street in front of the unit, wracking her brain trying to recall. Seeing the "#Sunshine" bumper sticker brought it all back.

The car belonged to Lois. What in the world was she doing here?

She whipped into the driveway, doing her best to not let anxiety overwhelm her, but quickly losing ground in that battle.

She pressed the doorbell, and then began knocking on the door right away. She shifted from one foot to the other, waiting for someone to answer.

Just before she could knock again, the front door opened. Confirming her theory, Lois stood in the entry. She was wearing the same clothes as last night.

Lois smiled, but dropped it as she saw the look on Viorica's face.

"Is...everything ok?" Lois called out to her.

"It's, um...is Maverick home?"

Lois shook her head. "He's out, I think he's looking for a church...do you want to come in?"

Vee froze for a second. She was already there, and slowly coming unhinged because of the unanswered questions. But she had to balance this against her desire not to intrude on whatever was happening.

"It's ok," Lois said, seeing her struggle to make the decision. "You can come in. You look like you have questions. I can probably help."

Vee decided to take her up on the offer. She stepped in.

Lois brought her to the glass kitchen table. There was already half a cup of coffee in the cartoon elephant mug.

"Would you like a cup? Fresh pot," Lois asked.

Viorica nodded, and Lois pulled out another mug for her.

"Just going to warm it up a bit," Lois said cheerfully. "I was using it to shoot a little content, so it got cold."

Vee raised an eyebrow. It sounded like Lois had an addiction, if she was making videos about her morning coffee. She tried not to judge too harshly.

"Sounds time-consuming," she said. Lois laughed and nodded.

"Oh, it is! But you gotta keep the content going, you know. Keep the fans engaged."

This made her pause. "Oh, so you're an actual influencer?"

Lois grinned as she poured the coffee. "You got it! My handle is Sunshine."

"That explains the bumper sticker," Vee said. She cocked her head to the side, trying to remember. "Shalyn used to talk about an influencer she followed all the time...I think it was Sunshine! That was you!"

Lois kept grinning, and nodded. "Sounds like it was. I've been doing it for a few years now."

"Wow. All this time, I never realized, or put it together. Is that how you know Maverick?"

"Oh no, I know him from the children's home. We were there together."

Vee watched her while taking a sip. "That's a crazy coincidence, then, that you both ended up here. But how did you end up *here*?" Vee motioned to the home around her.

"Maverick called me last night. He sounded upset, and asked me to come over to talk. He told me...well, he told me what's been going on. I crashed here overnight, because it was a lot. I think you'll want to hear the full story."

Viorica was relieved that there didn't seem to be romantic interest from Lois, at least not yet. And she was very interested in hearing the details.

"You know the story of what happened at the church?"

When Lois nodded, Vee followed up with: "Ok, so why was it an interim pastor who called him out? Why didn't the pastor at the time address it?"

Lois looked at her sadly. "That's the tragic part of the story. The pastor at the time, Pastor Waters, was involved in the situation."

Vee's eyes went wide.

Lois continued. "The woman Maverick had the affair with was Felicity. Felicity *Waters*. She was the pastor's wife."

Viorica had to set her cup down before she dropped it. This truth sent a shockwave through her.

She knew she couldn't let this change how she looked at Maverick. She was determined not to treat him like an exile and a criminal. But this introduced a whole new layer of nuance and complication to the situation.

And, it wasn't done.

"Waters," Viorica mumbled. "Pastor Waters..."

The color drained from her face, as the puzzle pieces began to lock together in her mind.

She remembered where she had heard that name.

"The church...is it still there?" Vee asked.

Lois shook her head. She looked like she was waiting, patiently, for Vee to understand.

"So, where...where was the church located, before it closed? What city?"

Lois reached out and took Viorica's hand. "Oak Hills," she said softly.

Vee gasped, and jumped to her feet. She understood at last.

"When I saw you last night, with Maverick, I didn't want to say anything," Lois said, sounding apologetic. "I figured you had ended things, and were looking for a new start, maybe. Or, that you knew, and didn't care, because that connection between the two of them was lost. Honestly, I don't know what I thought, besides that I should stay out of it."

Vee squeezed her hand. A tear ran down her face before she noticed, and absently she wiped it away.

"Now it makes sense why he was so conflicted last night, at least," she said. "And why his feelings changed after he learned my story."

"It does," Lois said, nodding her agreement. "He realized he was dating the woman his best friend was in love with."

"I was also a member of the Waters' church," Lois explained. "There were lots of us from the children's home around. The Nolan family brought all the kids they were raising with them, too. Any of us that were in need, the Waters took good care of us.

"When Felicity...when everything happened, it left scars on a lot of people. Everyone turned their backs on Maverick, because all the help and support we were getting, suddenly was gone."

"Nobody else in the church was willing to help?" Vee asked while standing. She wasn't able to sit back down yet.

"They were," Lois said. "But the Waters family was the most involved by far. And the person in the church who took it the hardest was Archer."

"They were friends?" Vee asked, but it was barely a question.

"*Best* friends," Lois said. "Even though Archie had a family, he and Maverick were like brothers."

Vee's hand trembled as she ran it through her hair.

"All this time..." she muttered. "I never knew..."

"Archie doesn't talk about things. It really messed him up. He had the Nolans, but they were way too busy. Every time a kid hit eighteen and moved out, they'd bring two more in. The church was his real home, and he thought it was his forever family."

Viorica chuckled as another tear fell. "I thought Maverick was playing dumb, calling him 'Archie'. You all call him that?"

Lois smiled. "He's always going to be Archie to us."

It felt like all the energy left her body. Vee took back her seat at last. She placed her head in her hands, and Lois shifted her chair next to her. She placed a comforting hand on Vee's shoulder.

They stayed silent for a long time, until Vee drew up the courage to ask what she had been wanting to know for months.

"How's...Archer doing? He's still at First Pentecostal?"

"He is! I have pictures, take a look!"

Lois' phone was out, and she began scrolling through the albums. She drew up full-screen pictures, and began swiping them to the side.

A collection of shots from before and after services. Various people and events at First Pentecostal. Viorica was able to recognize some right away.

Lois came across a sequence of photos of Archer. He looked to be thriving. His suits were upgraded to nicer fabrics, and Lois even had a few shots of him holding a microphone, giving a speech or sermon of some kind.

He looked like he belonged.

She swiped to a picture of Archer in the foreground, and another person next to him. Lois gasped and quickly swiped it away before Vee could make out the details.

She had a pretty good idea what it was, though.

"Go back, please," she asked softly. "it's ok."

Lois hesitated, but swiped back to the previous picture.

It was a close-up. Archer was side-by-side with a young woman. She had both arms around his shoulders.

Vee studied the woman in the picture. They were about the same age. The woman was beautiful, from any perspective. Her skin was flawless, rich as cocoa. Her teeth were dazzling white, and her curly hair was immaculately set in a flowing style.

"I know I've seen her somewhere before, but we've never met. I don't really know who she is," Lois hurriedly explained. She sounded apologetic again.

Vee's gaze lingered on the photo a few moments longer. "That's fine. I'm glad; they look happy. He's doing so well for himself there."

Only a single tear fell from her eye as she absorbed the info. Viorica took it as a sign she was ok.

Chapter 16

Viorica felt like she was drowning, with all she had learned in the past hour. While she appreciated having the clarity, she felt more confused than ever as to how she was going to proceed.

One thing stood out above all others: the church needed her. The Women's Ministry was in trouble, and they needed someone to help them get back on the course Alloise worked so hard to set.

After months upon months of drive, zeal, and longing, followed by pushing herself daily to let it all go, to forget everything she had worked for, Vee had finally found a place where, mentally, she was content.

The love she had for the church could not be, and had not been, completely extinguished by everything that had happened over the past six months.

Before, she knew there was a need for strong leadership. Now, the situation had become dire. It's like her eyes were opened, as she realized she didn't care anymore about roles. The fire she felt was still there, but it had transformed. If she could be a blessing by leading from within, then she would gladly give as much as she could from wherever she was.

That meant she had to go back to the church. And there were several key conversations that needed to be had.

Vee finished her coffee and took a deep breath. "Thank you for telling me the truth," she said to Lois. I have...a lot to think over."

Lois pulled her into a hug. "Don't be too mad at Maverick," she said. "He really does like you, I can tell. He thinks Archie will come around one day, and Maverick doesn't want anything to be between them when he does."

Vee saved Lois' number to her phone, and went back home.

She felt like she needed to lie down, but she had some strategizing to do. The first thing she did after she got home was bring out all the office supplies she had: pens, notepads, index cards, staplers, all the odds and ends she had accumulated from her job.

She brought her materials out to the living room. She didn't want to be there, and avoided it as often as possible while at home, but it had the most space for what she needed to do.

She stood in front of the love seat. She remembered one of the last times she spent with Archer.

They had been on the balcony, trying to make conversation about anything besides church. For weeks he had tried to convince her to come back with him the next Sunday, while she repeatedly made it clear that the topic was not up for discussion.

After they had failed to come up with anything interesting to talk about, Viorica opened the door to her apartment.

"Come in," she had said. "Let's watch a movie."

He raised his eyebrows. "Vee, I...I can't be in your apartment alone with you."

She snapped her head up, eyes blazing. "Why not?" she had demanded. "Are you afraid somebody's watching, and going to tell on us? What else are they going to do, ex-communicate me?!"

Her voice had traveled, deliberately, across the courtyard. Archer had hurried in, only wanting to appease her.

They sat together, Viorica with her knees curled up to her chest as she reclined against him. She didn't even remember the movie they watched, she was so lost in her anger. She saw the sadness on Archer's face, and couldn't even bring herself to talk to him. Altogether, it was a miserable night for them both.

She dried fresh tears from her eyes at the memory. Then, she took a seat, and got to work.

For hours she filled out index cards, jotted down notes of what she knew, worked on putting pieces together. She didn't have all the data, being apart from the church for so long. There were elements that would have to fall in place in time. But whatever she knew, she noted and added to her strategy. She opened the city of Ocala's website on her phone and scrolled through the calendar of events.

Hours ticked away as she refined the plan. Once she had it on paper, she powered up her computer and began to document it into a formal proposal.

Finally, she saved the file and closed the laptop. She knew the next step was to get the proposal to the people that could put it into motion.

And the one person who had the most say, besides the pastor, had waited long enough to hear from her.

Vee's hand trembled as she scrolled through the contacts. She didn't know what she was going to say, but she knew it was time.

She held her breath as the phone rang.

"Hello?" A woman's voice answered on the third ring. It was light, too young to be Alloise. Viorica almost didn't recognize it, until...

"Hi...is this Shalyn?!"

"Hi Vee! Yes, it's me."

Hearing her voice produced a tugging in her chest. Shalyn had lost her adopted country twang from last year. She was growing into an adult voice, thanks to the formal Connecticut accent she naturally carried.

"Oh my God, Shalyn, it's been so long! You sound like a grown woman!"

Shalyn laughed a little on the other end. "It has been a while. Where have you been, Vee?'

She felt oceans of shame rocking her. "I was in a pretty bad place," she admitted. "I don't know if you heard about what happened…"

"I heard," Shalyn said. Her voice was soft. "When Aunt Alloise recovered from her surgery in June, she was asking for you. She cried, a lot, when they told her."

Hearing it made new tears form in Vee's eyes as well.

"What did she say about it?"

"Nothing, I don't think. They would not tell me, because I was just a kid. *Am* just a kid. But I know Aunt Alloise has been asking to see you."

"Is she able to have visitors?" Vee grabbed her car keys as she asked. "I guess not if you're answering her phone?"

"One moment please, let me check." Shalyn audibly put the phone down. Distantly, Vee heard her voice, and the voice of several others. It was impossible to make out the words, but when Shalyn came back to the phone, she said:

"Aunt Alloise really wants to see you."

That's was all Vee needed. The moment Shalyn gave her the address, she was heading to her car.

Vee checked in at the security desk enclosed in glass just outside the lobby. As soon as she walked through the doors, Shalyn was there, with a tall woman who looked like an older version of her.

Shayln jumped into Vee's arms. Vee squeezed her tiny body, marveling at how she'd grown almost a full foot.

She introduced herself to the woman, LaShay, Shalyn's mother and Alloise's niece. She also greeted Vee with a warm hug.

"Aunt Ally talks about you all the time," she explained, leading them into the building.

"I'm sorry I didn't come sooner," Vee said. She kept her eyes on the floor as they stepped into the elevator.

Shalyn grabbed Vee's hand while her mother smiled at her. "It's ok. You're here now." LaShay told her.

Together they approached the room. Vee took a deep breath before stepping inside.

Alloise was in a mobility chair, parked by the window. She was drawing in prolonged, wheezing breaths as she stared out over the sunlit lawn.

Shaking, Vee let go of Shalyn's hand and approached the woman who had been a mother to her for years.

"Hi, Ma," she said in a strained whisper.

Alloise turned in her chair. She dropped the crochet hooks she was absently fidgeting with. Her mouth fell open, and tears immediately began falling from her jaundiced eyes.

Vee could barely see, beyond her own tears, Alloise struggle to raise her arms, beckoning her forward.

She closed the distance in a run. Sobbing, she fell on Alloise's shoulder. She felt the frail woman's arms embrace her with all her might, which was considerable given her condition.

The two women held the embrace, crying out sorrow of the past several months. Healing tears wet both of their shirts.

When Vee finally pulled herself up, she kissed Alloise on the forehead while she fought to compose herself. Alloise handed her a cloth to clean her face, and produced a second one for herself.

"Ma, I'm sorry, I should have came sooner—" Alloise patted her arm to silence her words.

"You're here now," she whispered, echoing her niece's words. Vee's smile beamed as she pulled up a chair next to her.

"When everything happened...they told me you couldn't have visitors, and by the time you had recovered, I was so ashamed, because I wasn't going to church..."

Alloise shook her head, as fiercely as she could. "I wanted to see you. I tried to fight for you, but the vote had already gone through. I needed..." Alloise turned aside and fell into a coughing fit. Once it subsided, she took several deep breaths before she continued.

"I needed, to make sure you were ok," she said. A hand reached out to grab Vee by the arm.

"I'm sorry," Alloise said, her eyes spilling over again. "Sorry I couldn't be there for you. And that you had no one to..."

It was Viorica's turn to shake her head. She wrapped Alloise in a tight hug again.

"No, Ma, it's not your fault at all. You needed to get better, because we need you here with us."

The embrace lasted as long as before. When Vee sat back down, Alloise glanced down at the ink letter and numbers on her forearm. Vee noticed, and also saw that Alloise still looked at her with nothing but love.

Just knowing she knew made Vee self-conscious. In vain, she pulled at the sleeve of her shirt, which was nowhere near long enough to cover it up.

"I got it a couple months ago," she hastily explained. "it's actually from—"

"I know," Alloise said with a nod and a smile. "I understand; it's part of your story."

She patted her leg, and Vee took her hand again.

"So, when are they letting you out of here?" she asked. "We've got work to do at the church. I already know they haven't been keeping up on your filing system."

Alloise made a wheezing sound, from deep in her chest. "Don't," she said, waving a frail hand. "Hurts to laugh."

LaShay stepped over, just behind Vee. "Right now, they're trying to monitor the fatigue, make sure she's able to be awake consistently. We also want to make sure there's no kidney failure, and that we keep any infections away."

Vee nodded. "What do you need me to do? I can help get the house set up for when she's ready to come back home."

LaShay smiled and gave a grateful nod. "I'll be sure to coordinate with you, we would appreciate it."

"You have something else to do," Alloise interjected, motioning at Vee. "The Women's Ministry is in trouble. Losing members. They need you to help them get back on track."

Viorica sighed. "I know. I have a plan, I have the proposal. I just need them to put it all into action.

"I don't care about being the head anymore. I just want the ministry to succeed. How do I get them to listen to me long enough to do what I'm suggesting?"

Alloise pointed a finger at her. It felt like she was pointing directly to her soul.

"You get back in church!" she said, with all the force in her body behind her words.

Maverick came walking through his front door just as Lois finished editing and uploading her latest video. She was moving to wash the cartoon elephant mug in the sink.

"Any luck?" she called out to him. Maverick came and stood in the kitchen.

"I did find a church that seems promising," he said. "I'll have to see how it goes."

Lois said nothing while she waited for him to ask.

"So...did Vee...?"

"She was here," Lois said. "I told her the whole story, she knows everything."

With an exhale, Maverick came and wrapped one arm around Lois' shoulders.

"That's a relief, thank you."

"It really should have been you," she said. "I think she really likes you. You can build something real with her."

Maverick shook his head. "Not until I fix things with Archie." He left the kitchen to change out of his Sunday attire.

Unknown to both of them, at the time, Lois' latest video, a simple twenty-second clip talking about life in Ocala, went viral, thanks to the adorable coffee mug.

Crowds began flocking to novelty stores and websites, looking for their own version. The manufacturer saw the spike in web searches of their product, and received an analytics report, tracing it back to the post that triggered the spike. By that time the next day, they would reach out to the creator, Sunshine, and offer her a promotion deal and free merchandise.

The popularity of the post meant it received a boost across the social media platform. People who otherwise wouldn't have found it coming across their feed.

One particular man, just outside of Orlando, saw it. He immediately recognized the cup, and recognized who it belonged to.

The internet had done the work for him. He now knew where to look.

Act 3

Chapter 17

Picture: a woman strong in her faith, with confidence renewed, and a restored connection to her God-given purpose. Viorica spent her work week fine-tuning her strategy. When she wasn't called to prep or retrieve documents, she was planning her approach on how to save the ministry.

All the messages had been sent. All the contacts were in place. Everything seemed to come down to Emma and Michelle. For better or for worse, they were the gatekeepers. She had to convince them that her plan was worth putting into action. It also meant that there was going to have to be a talk between the three of them. Apologies and rebukes were expected all around.

She couldn't help but wonder what she would say to Archer when she got back in church. He was definitely owed an apology; she just couldn't fathom expressing herself the way she needed without crossing any boundaries with his potential relationship. Who knew where his mind was these days?

The best thing she could do was put her future in God's hands and focus on the next steps. If she had to let Archer go for now, then that's what she would do.

Friday came and went. Viorica dropped off the last stack of forms she was dealing with, and started getting ready to leave.

Cheryl came up behind her. "TGIF! Ready for the Dressage wine-tasting tour?"

Vee tied on her coat. "Not this weekend, I'm afraid. Got other plans."

Cheryl raised an eyebrow. "But you've been talking about this for months! You find something more important?"

"I sure did," she said with a smirk.

She left work and set her sights on the first step:

First Pentecostal Church.

Vee didn't anticipate how it would feel, coming back after so long. She started to park in one of her usual spaces, but thought better of it.

She turned off her engine and stared at the building that had meant so much to her over the past few years. She had gone from being consumed with love for her church, to desperately pretending it never existed in an effort to make the hurt she experienced vanish.

This was the first time in months she would step foot in First Pentecostal. She wasn't entirely sure the hurt had healed yet. A substantial part of her wanted to stay away, remembering the very moment when everything turned to ash in front of her eyes.

Vee took a breath and said a prayer. She felt the hand of God around her. That was all she needed to be bold. She approached the front door, and walked in with her head held high.

Her steps took her into the sanctuary. She passed the same row of pews where she had sat, face in hand, learning that she was to be sat down right before the vote. On the opposite side, she passed the seats where Emma and Michelle sat, refusing to look at her, maybe smiling, maybe crying.

It didn't matter anymore. She could carry the hurt for a little while longer.

She crossed the hall to the pastor's office and knocked on the door. Angelica Flores opened and greeted her with an immediate hug.

"Sister Vee, we have missed you!"

Vee returned the hug. "Thank you, Sister Angelica. It's so good to see you again."

"Please, come with me."

She led Vee to an office adjacent to the pastor's office. This space was decorated with plush armchairs, a small end table, and shelves of various books. Vee sat in one of the armchairs at Angelica's suggestion.

"I know you had your meeting scheduled with Samuel. But, when I heard you wanted to speak with him, I asked if I could speak with you first."

She sat in the other chair with a sweet smile, and sincerity in her eyes.

"I wanted to apologize," she told Vee. "I should have spoken up. When you left, we knew it was because of what happened. I wanted to reach out to you sooner, but Samuel said to let you come around on your own. I...disagreed, but I trust him."

Viorica didn't know, if Angelica had reached out, whether it would make her feel better or not. All she said was: "You're fine. I had a lot to deal with."

"But you shouldn't have had to deal with it alone. What happened was not right. The least we could have done was support you through it. You have given so much to this church."

Angelica's words were cutting closer and closer to her heart. Vee could only nod as she took them in.

"Would you tell me your story, please? What happened in the past year while you were away?"

That, she could do.

Vee told her the story of the dark times she spent wallowing in her desolation. She Showed her the tattoo, told her about the many, many nights spent on barstools.

She told a brief summary of how she met a guy who turned out to be a Christian himself, and how his story convinced her to shake off the hurt. She didn't mention Maverick's name, or much of his life.

Vee devoted the majority of her time to talking about how she learned that Lois, an influencer, had been coming to First Pentecostal, and how they were missing out on a key contact that would help revitalize the church.

Angelica listened to it all, but visibly perked up once Vee began talking about the Women's Ministry.

"This is why we need you!" Angelica said, sitting forward in her seat. "We need to take advantage of our resources more. The ministry is struggling to come up with fresh ideas. We can maintain, and keep it all the same, but we need to make plans to grow."

"And I have a way for us to do that," Vee said. "I came to realize: my love for this church wasn't based on potentially being head of a ministry. If the church needs help, and I have a way to help, I want to. I don't care who's in charge, I just want to see everything Alloise built thrive again."

Sister Flores was beaming. "You have a plan, and you're willing to share it with us?"

Viorica nodded. "I know it may not be received well, coming from me, but I have to be able to say I offered it."

"You are exactly who we want to hear from," Angelica said as she stood. "Your name is brought up in every ministry meeting. We've been waiting for you."

Vee was genuinely stunned.

"Waiting for me?" she echoed. Angelica nodded and opened the office door, ushering Vee out. As they walked down the hall, they saw the door to pastor's office was open. Angelica turned inside, and Vee followed.

Pastor Flores was waiting, with Emma and Michelle in the seat waiting as well.

This ought to be good, Vee thought to herself.

She was unsure what to expect from the meeting. For a solid five seconds, nobody said anything.

The standoff ended with Michelle plodding over to Vee, and hugging her shoulders tightly.

It was certainly the last thing she was expecting.

"You've been so missed," Michelle said while holding on to her. Vee frowned, and patted Michelle on the back as the hug drew on longer and longer.

Michelle finally stepped away when Pastor Flores cleared his throat.

"Sister Vee, thank you for coming here today," he said. "Let me start by saying, you were missed indeed."

"What happened was painful," Vee said, not mincing the words. "It took me a very long time to get to the place I am now. But the church needs a new approach, and I have ideas, so I couldn't sit by and do nothing. In the past, leading a ministry was the most important thing to me. Now, I just want to help."

She looked over at her two former friends. "Things were strained between us," she said to both of them. "I don't know who said what, or what any intentions were, but I know that I'm equally responsible for letting the relationship lapse. So, for that, I am sorry."

Emma shook her head. "It's my fault as well. When I ran into you downtown last week, I couldn't put into words what happened, or how I felt. I hope you believed what I said about not intentionally trying to sabotage you."

"Same here," Michelle said. "You have strengths in every single area Emma and I are weak. You're the best of us, and we really can't do this ministry without you."

Vee's jaw dropped. It was the most personable thing Michelle had ever said. Not to mention the most profound.

"I, um, I'm flattered," Viorica admitted. "But I want to be clear: I'm not trying to buy my way into a ministry. I'm only here to help."

"We'll take all the help you can give," pastor said. "I received your email with the proposal, and I'll admit, I have a lot of questions. Can you explain it to us?"

Vee grinned . "Of course I can. Let's start with the city fair, next weekend..."

Chapter 18

Vee never would have thought her wild idea would have been such a raging success. Yet, as she stood in the field after the city fair, with the late evening wind gently pushing away the heat and the tension of the day, she took a look around, and saw it was so.

According to the records she was given, there were no less than one hundred people who signed up to receive information about the church. At least twenty-five people followed the church's brand new social media page. Fifty families RSVP'd for the next church dinner that was to be held the first Sunday of next month. They even had fifteen people who signed up to be baptized in the coming week.

Vee took a seat, for the first time in hours, and let out a sigh of relief. The plan, which had maybe four days to execute, had fallen into place perfectly. Lois' social media reach proved to be the game-changer, as anticipated.

It was a massive victory, but Viorica still felt empty.

Angelica took a seat in a folding chair next to her. "We did it," she said with a grin. She searched Viorica's face, openly trying to gauge her mood.

Vee tried to return the smile as best she could. "Thank God, we did," she said quietly.

Angelica kept patient eyes on her, waiting for Vee to express what was on her mind. She stayed tight-lipped, so Angelica filled in the blanks for her.

"You're still thinking about Archer?"

Angelica had hit the nail on the head.

After the Friday meeting at the church, Pastor Flores asked the important question, one that everyone in the room wanted to know: would Viorica be at the Sunday morning service that week?

In the few seconds she thought about it, Vee was struck with a sudden homesickness so profound, the answer was easy. The waves on the sea of shame that battered her for so long had abated to perfectly becalmed. For the first time in months, she felt she was no longer floundering while trying to tread water.

She was ready to come home. She told them all yes, she would attend the church service.

They cheered. They hugged her. Pastor prayed for the Women's Ministry, and everyone in the room. Viorica went home to make sure she still had church clothes that survived her closet purge.

When she awoke, 7 a.m. sharp, she made it halfway through her familiar Sunday morning routine before she realized she would see Archer again that day.

She still hadn't been able to bring herself to text, or call, him. She knew she wouldn't be able to handle his consternation, or his rejection. If he mentioned that he was happy with the incredible woman who loved taking close pictures with him, she would have died, with no armor for her wounded heart.

The apprehension slowed her steps, but she determined not to let it stop her. She packed up and went out into the brisk morning, eyes fixed on the house of worship.

When she arrived, she immediately began greeting people she hadn't seen since her last service. Archer was among the ones there early to set up.

She saw him. He clearly saw her. Their eyes locked, and the unspoken emotions flowed between them.

But he turned away, and didn't say a word to her.

The reality was somehow worse than everything she feared.

Viorica tried to let it go. She tried to connect, to engage with the message, and to give God her full attention after so much time away.

She succeeded, while service was going on. The minute they were dismissed, she began making her way over to where Archer was sitting.

He skillfully slipped through a crowd and was gone.

It ached. The situation was even more difficult, but Vee had no choice but to carry it. There was so much to do that she had no spare time or energy to devote to falling to pieces because of him.

So, the plan for the city fair went into action. Because they hadn't registered as vendors, they had to do guerilla-style outreach: t-shirts from an event several years ago for all the volunteers. Community engagers spread strategically around the fairgrounds. Small printed literature that advertised the church and directed people where to go to learn more. Emma and Michelle took point securing these details.

Viorica had spent almost every day after work with Lois, setting up the new social media platform, and strategizing what sort of content they would need. Shooting, editing, scripting, learning how to make an effective post, all delivered in a crash course.

When the day of the fair came, everyone played their part to perfection. It was a symphony of activity, and everything worked exactly as it needed for the primary goal to be met: bring people into the church, so they can be pointed to Jesus Christ.

In-between live streaming at the event, Vee bounced around the different stations. She helped Michelle keep track of the paperwork, and introduced her to Alloise's organization system. She then drifted over to help Emma, who was holding on-the-spot interviews and contests for the social media page with every willing participant.

Even Pastor and Angelica Flores had roles. They purchased bulk orders of water, coffee, tea, and lemonades from the fair vendors and sat at a table in one of the tents. They gave out a free beverage to anyone who wanted to sit and chat, and every conversation they had turned into the Gospel message of hope in Christ.

Archer was there too, that day. The first time Viorica saw him, she had been congratulating a gentleman on passing Emma's Bible trivia contest. The man, with bleary, hollow eyes, a growing patchwork of unkempt facial hair, and a ball cap tucked low over his head, wore faded jeans and a flannel shirt. He claimed to not be a believer, or have any religious background, but he answered all four questions of Emma's Bible trivia right away.

Viorica brought him his prize, a water bottle with the church logo, and peeked over his shoulder to see Archer.

Her face fell, and she tried to decide if she was going to approach him or not. The man declined the offer and headed out of the fairgrounds to an old blue pickup truck that was parked nearby. Once he was gone, she began striding over to Archer, who went off to some other part of the fair.

All day, she kept looking for him, hoping that he would end the silence and approach her. Or, at the very least, for him to pass by close enough for her to take the first step and approach him.

She got no other glances of him. As things began to shut down, and the crowds dwindled, she made rounds further and further out from the center of the area the church had claimed. She came away empty-handed each time.

Vee folded her arms on the table and laid her head down on top of them. To Viorica from last year, an event this successful would have had her on cloud-nine. This would have cemented her leadership role. But the Viorica she was, in that moment, felt hollow. Everything amounted to a meaningless victory.

Angelica patted her gently on the back, and left to find Pastor Flores. Vee lifted her head to survey what needed to be done.

The light was fading into twilight, and the majority of people were already gone. The vendors who had sold out were closing their booths and packing up supplies. Crowds of people were laughing as they socialized with one another. Vee saw, absently, that the old blue pickup truck was still circling the fairgrounds. The driver seemed to be in a daze.

She was about to start heading for the exit, when Maverick appeared with a smile.

Viorica gasped as she saw him. "What are you doing here?!"

"Enjoying the fair," he said with a laugh. He wore a light cotton hoodie and cargo pants, and more of that enchanting cologne. "It's been a while since I heard from you."

Vee felt a twinge of guilt, but not enough to make her feel like she was drowning on the sea of shame anymore. "Sorry, I had a lot to do to pull this off."

"Lois told me," Maverick said with a nod. "You two have really been nose to the grindstone on this!"

"You have no idea."

Maverick reached out, smoothly, and took her hand. Vee did a double take when she realized what he had done.

"We have a lot to talk about," he said, low and kindly. "I should probably apologize—"

"No, it's ok. You said it best; there's a lot to unpack." She couldn't shake the apprehension of being seen in public with a love interest. The trauma of last time was still speaking to her.

Not to mention, this would be the *worst* time imaginable for Archer to decide to come her way.

"There is. But Vee, I have to let you know, you're important to me. Whether you decide to pursue something with me, or if you want to try again with Archie…Archer, you'll always be important to me."

She was genuinely touched, but still needed to change the look of this situation as soon as possible. She smiled and patted his hand, warmly.

"Thank you," she said. "It means a lot. I still need to have a conversation with Archer, but I haven't found him yet—"

She was trying to peel her hand away when she heard the last voice she wanted to hear, coming from behind her:

"So, looks like you haven't changed."

All day, Viorica had been praying in her heart:

Lord, let him look at me. Let him see me, let him find me. Let him notice me.

But at that moment, her prayers changed to one simple, clear message:

Lord, let him be far, far away from here.

Before she even spun around, she knew it was him.

Maverick dropped her hand as he faced his best friend.

"Hey Archie. How's it going?"

Maverick stepped forward, extending his arm for a handshake.

Vee flinched as Archer smacked his hand away.

"What are you doing here?" Archer's voice was almost a growl.

Maverick's pain was written all over his face. "I'm just here to support a friend, man."

Archer's hands clenched into fists. He stayed rooted in place. "You sure you're not here to ruin something else for me?! Trying to bring down another home I've found?"

Viorica wasn't sure, at first, whether to stay between them, or to get out of the way. The choice became clear when she saw Archer curl his fists, and launch that accusation.

"Archer, that's not fair..."

He turned to look at Viorica for just a moment. She saw plenty of anger, as well as the hurt he carried, rising and spilling over.

"Better be careful, Vee," Archer said to her. His tone held an edge of mockery in it. "You can't trust this guy. You let him in, he'll ruin everything you love!'

Vee stood her ground, frowning. "Don't you dare vilify him and try to pretend it's because you care about me," she snapped. "You've been avoiding me all week, and now you want to use me to take shots at him? I don't think so!"

The two men had locked eyes again. Viorica wasn't even sure Archer was still listening. Archer's were glaring, while Maverick's were pleading.

"Archie, come on. How long are you going to be angry at me? I've repented, I've done what I can to make it right—!"

Archer closed the distance in a half step, and shoved Maverick back.

"Don't talk like I'm the one who broke things!" He bellowed. "You haven't done *a thing* to make it right!"

Maverick planted his foot to stop from staggering back. He grunted, wanting to put his hands up in response, but kept them at his side.

Vee noticed that people all over the fairgrounds were staring in this direction. The vendors had stopped closing up their booths, and were watching carefully in case there was big trouble.

No cars were moving. The blue pickup truck had stopped.

Vee put herself between the two of them again.

"Archer, stop it! Don't put your hands on him."

He kept glaring, but this time turned to the side to level his glare on her.

"So, you're with him now?"

"Don't you dare!" Vee felt herself turning bright red as she took a step to get in Archer's face.

"Don't you dare go throwing out insinuations like that! You have no right! Especially after I've seen pictures with you and somebody else!"

He narrowed his eyes, confused, but didn't say anything. She kept going as her anger fully surfaced.

"I've been trying to connect with you since I got back in church," she said. "I've had to watch you ignore me, turn your back on me for the past two weeks! You do not get to use me as ammunition against your friend!"

"My 'friend'?" Archer said with a scoff. "Do you even know what he did? What being his friend cost me?!"

"Yes, I know," she said, trying to soften his tone with hers. "I know the story. I think it's time to talk it out. You two have to have a conversation. You and I do too."

Archer's fists stayed clenched, but Vee could see the change come over him. It started with the look in his eyes, and then followed by the tense frown he wore fading off his face. He took deep breaths, each one slower than the last.

Vee smiled a little as he de-escalated. She looked at Maverick to make sure he was likewise calming down.

She was startled by the sudden look of confusion on Maverick's face. At first, she thought it was directed at Archer.

Then, as his confusion turned to panic, Vee realized Maverick was looking past Archer.

She turned to see what it was. As soon as she turned, someone came barreling between her and Archer, knocking him aside and her to the ground.

She tumbled as she met the grass. Dazed, she looked up to see the man from the fair, with the scruffy beard and faded jeans tackle Maverick, taking them both to the ground.

Chapter 19

M averick hit the ground rolling to keep the sudden stranger off of him.

They tumbled together, a flurry of limbs thrashing out every direction.

Vee propped herself up by her elbows. She went pale, watching the two flail about.

Some of the fairgoers were looking on in shock. A few had their phones out and were recording. One looked as if they had dialed the authorities.

She felt a strong hand grab her by the arm and begin to lift her, carefully, to her feet. She saw Archer at her side.

"Are you ok?!" he demanded, eyes on the fight.

Viorica nodded, and the moment she did, Archer let her go and rushed over to break up the exchange.

The strange man had wrestled Maverick beneath him. His fists were raining down. Maverick's hands were up protecting his head and face.

"You stole my family! Stole everything!" The strange man bellowed as he hammered at Maverick's body wherever he could.

"Jason!" Archer cried out before he grabbed the man. He managed to drag him to the side, allowing Maverick to clamber to his feet.

The man pushed against Archer, a mad glare in his weary eyes. They had locked hands and were exerting to push the other back.

"You...little...!"

The man gave a titanic shove, bending Archer's arms back. Using the range of motion, he brought his elbow forward to meet Archer's jaw.

The strike had little power, but disoriented Archer enough that he stumbled. He fell back a couple steps before he saved his footing.

While he was recovering, the man reached into his waist for something. Vee couldn't see it, only the trail of his arm as he lashed out.

Archer's cry of pain made her skin grow cold.

Viorica gasped, and screamed unintentionally as she watched Archer clutch his side and fall to a knee.

The man, Jason, turned towards Maverick, brandishing a large hunting knife.

Maverick had his hands up, and was furiously backpedaling to give himself space.

"Pastor Waters, please, stop!" Maverick yelled.

Vee gasped. It all made horrible sense.

She knew this man was going to kill Maverick. She had to stop him.

'In Jesus' Name...' Vee prayed

Just as Jason Waters began to lunge, Vee got to her feet and sprinted to intercept them.

She stood in front of him, with her arms out to the side. Archer and Maverick both began shouting for her to get out of there, but she stood firm.

Thankfully, Jason stopped his charge, staring blankly at her.

"Out of my way," he said.

Viorica shook her head. "I won't. Pastor Waters, you need to stop."

"I'm not a pastor anymore!' he whipped the knife around as he screamed.

"That ungrateful bastard," he pointed the tip of the knife at Maverick, who was slowly moving from behind Viorica and circling around, "tore my family apart! I took him in, and he stole my wife. He cost me my marriage and my role as pastor!"

"What Maverick did was wrong," Viorica said. She began moving as well, keeping Maverick in her periphery so she could stand between him and the ex-pastor. "My heart goes out to you. But, even though you may not have the role of pastor, in God's eyes you are still loved. You *both* are loved. This behavior is not befitting a child of God, sir."

Jason Waters planted his feet and tightened his grip on his knife.

"You've fallen for him," he said, shaking his head. "He put you under some sort of spell, the same spell he used on my wife, and now he's hiding behind you while you defend him!"

"He has done no such thing! I'm your sister in Christ, only trying to remind you that you are better than this!"

Vee could hear the sirens of first responders approaching. She estimated three minutes before they got here.

Three minutes, however, was plenty of time for anything to happen.

"Get out of my way, girl," Jason said again. His voice dropped lower than before. "I won't ask again."

Even though her knees felt weak, and her heart pounded, Vee shook her head. In the corner of her eye, she saw Maverick moving forward to stand next to her.

With a scoff, Jason lunged again. He was less than twenty feet away, closing quick.

Time seemed to slow. Vee felt Maverick's hand on her shoulder, firmly pushing her out of the path of Jason Waters' knife.

She didn't dare blink, lest she miss something.

The world turned sideways as she fell, for the second time that day, onto the grass, landing on her shoulder.

She saw Jason's evil grin as he closed in on Maverick, who was bracing himself.

At the last second, Archer came from the side, like a dart.

He dropped his shoulder and ran into Jason full-force, knocking him to the ground.

Jason landed with a heavy *thud*, and the knife went flying free from his hands.

Viorica saw it tumble into the grass, just as the police came rushing in towards the scene.

Officers began to pick the men up, separating them for questioning. Two officers grabbed Jason Waters and restrained him as he raged and thrashed.

When a uniformed officer stood over her and helped her to her feet, Vee finally allowed herself to blink.

Chapter 20

P olice interviews were wrapped up quickly. Multiple eye-witnesses, along with several phone recordings, showed Jason Waters as the aggressor. After the police gathered his statement, Jason went from bellowing to silent.

Viorica watched as they handcuffed him and placed him in the back of a squad car. He looked out into the crowds of people at the fairground, and she saw the defeated look in his eyes before they closed the car door. Despite the terror of the past few moments, she felt a fresh tug at her heartstrings for him.

She gave the officer her statement in a daze. She had a quick examination from the paramedics and was cleared right away. She kept the cotton blanket they draped over her shoulders as she walked off, trying to find who was left from church.

Emma, Michelle, and Lois all were gone. Pastor Flores was gone as well. Vee thought to grab her phone and call him, but then she realized it had been lost in all the excitement and was nowhere to be found.

Her nerves beyond frazzled, she had the thought to ask Archer to help her find it. She began to head towards the ambulance that was examining him.

It startled her to see him sitting on the gurney in the back, and the paramedics closing the door.

"No...Archer!" she began to run towards him, bewildered. She felt someone grab her by the waist and hold her back.

It took her several moments to recognize Maverick.

"Let me go! I need..."

He shushed her, still holding firm to her waist to stop her from running. "It's ok. He's fine, he just had a scratch. They're taking him to the hospital to get it looked at and stitched up."

She wanted to protest, but then she looked at Maverick's face. She saw the bruises that were already beginning to form there.

"You're hurt too," she said. Her voice was flat from the letdown of adrenaline.

"It's fine," he said with an attempt at his trademark smile. "It only hurts when I move too fast. Or laugh, or breathe."

The adrenaline continued to drain from her body, and she felt increasingly weak. She said nothing as her legs began to wobble.

Maverick caught this and half-led, half-carried her to one of the nearby folding chairs. He sat her down gently and replaced the blanket over her shoulders.

He took a deep breath as he sat in a chair next to her. "I...I owe you big time, Viorica. I'm so sorry you got involved in this mess, and I hate myself for putting you in it. But I don't know what would have happened today if you weren't there. Thank you."

She had regained enough clarity to be present for the conversation. She reached a shaky hand up and placed it on his cheek.

"You're a good man, Maverick," she said softly.

He closed his eyes and covered her hand on his face with his own. She saw the tear fall, heard the ragged breath as he inhaled.

"I'm really not," he said, refusing to look at her. "I brought all this on myself, and I dragged a bunch of other people into it too. I ruined an entire family, lost my best friend, almost got him killed..."

Wordless, she pulled him into a close hug. He wrapped both arms around her as he fell onto her shoulder.

She let him cry out his frustrations, his pain. She felt it in his muscles, through his chest, as the anguish vented from his soul. Once his sobs stopped and his breathing returned to normal, she pulled him back to look at him. He hurriedly tried to clean and fix his face as she did.

"You were just as much a victim as anyone," she said. "You've learned, you've grown, and most importantly, you've kept your connection with God. He has already forgiven you, now it's time to forgive yourself."

His eyes fell from hers, but he nodded as he tried to internalize her words. She gave him a light kiss on the cheek. It felt lifting to her, to share a tiny bit of the affection she knew he had been starving for.

Viorica approached the reception desk of the hospital. The harried nurse greeted her with a smile while typing furiously.

"Hi! Can I help you?"

"Yes, I'm here to see a new patient, Archer Nolan?"

The nurse turned towards the screen. After several mouse clicks and keyboard strokes, she looked up and told Viorica the room number.

Vee made her way to the room and knocked.

She peeked inside to see Archer in a bed that had been set up to the reclining position. He glanced toward the door, and his smile lit up her soul.

"Hey," he said, shifting to sit up even further.

"Hey," Vee echoed. She sat on the edge of the bed, facing him.

"I didn't get a chance to check on you before they wheeled me off. Are you alright?" His face suddenly morphed as heavy concern blanketed his features.

She patted him on the leg. "I'm fine, no worries. It's actually because of *you* I'm fine."

His relief was visible. "Thank you, God," he said, closing his eyes before meeting hers again. "If something had happened to you, I don't know what I would..."

His voice trailed off. She came up next to him and gave him a careful hug, avoiding his wounded side.

She let the hug linger and found her heart racing. Not just from the thrill of being near him again, she noticed, but something else. All of the unspoken words that she had meant to share with him were fighting to be heard. She realized, if something had happened to *him*, she would probably be out on the sea of shame forever.

She didn't want to risk that ever again. Tears welled up as she buried her face against him.

"I could have lost you," she said. The realization was dominating all other thoughts.

"You didn't" he spoke in undertone. "God kept us safe."

"I know, but..." she sat up. She held his face in both of her hands, softly. She gazed into those metallic blue eyes again, and the familiar warmth suffused her.

"Archer, I can't tell you how sorry I am," she began. "You met me when I was at my lowest. I was horrible to you, and it was so unfair for me to put you through that, all because of what I was facing."

He shook his head. "No, Vee. It was because of me that you didn't get into the ministry. I tried to make up for it when we were dating, but I felt so guilty it was all I could think about.

"When I saw you back at the church...I didn't know how to feel. I thanked God that you were back, but I didn't know if you were trying again. I made myself stay away so I wouldn't hurt your chances—"

"That's not who I am anymore," she said, a sad smile on her face. "I let my desire to be in ministry consume me, to the point where I was failing relationships with people around me. When my chances at a leadership role were gone, I was devastated because it felt like I had nothing left to lean on. I'm trying a different way. I'm just going to do what I can to help, and let God use me wherever He wants."

Archer nodded. He started to say something, but Vee felt like she knew what it was going to be, and had to get ahead of the heartbreak.

"If you're with someone else, I won't stand in your way." She dropped her hands and her gaze at the same time.

"What do you mean?" he asked.

"I saw the picture. That gorgeous woman you took a picture with on Lois' page..."

He frowned. She looked back up at him, confused.

"That beautiful woman who was hanging over you! Flawless brown skin, curly hair!"

"Oh, you mean Lisa!" He laughed, and then gasped and clutched his side.

Vee didn't know whether to smack him or comfort him, so she froze.

"Who...who's Lisa?"

"Lisa Nolan, my sister. She grew up with me. She lives in Tampa, she came to church with me that day."

With that, the last bit of tension Viorica had been carrying evaporated from her body.

"It's only you," he said, his voice heavy with his deepest emotions. She met his eyes once again. "You're the only one I've been after. I've prayed day and night since you left, that God would bring you back to me. Now—"

She didn't wait for him to finish.

There was no split-second tease, no whispers of a kiss this time. She put her whole soul into it.

She felt the voltage race through her again, warming the cold places of her heart. The areas of her being that she had closed off from the world suddenly sprang to new life.

She inhaled him, imprinting his very being on her spirit. She locked her heart with his, knowing that he was her future, and that God had called them to be.

Chapter 21

"Sister Vee, that sounds like an unbelievable night."

Pastor Flores had no idea how right he was.

"My wife and I left as everything was closing down. I'm so sorry I was not there. Thank God Archer was, and everyone ended up safe."

He sat down at his desk, across from Viorica who sat in the office chair.

She wore a simple blouse and chemise, with a brand-new, full-length skirt. She strongly considered a jacket for the meeting, to cover her tattoo, but in the very end, she decided against it.

She had let shame dictate her actions, and even her thoughts, for far too long. She had wasted too much life trying to repress her feelings, then trying to forget where she came from. All she received for her efforts was the feeling of being further lost, adrift on the sea of shame.

No longer would she live on that sea. It was time to explore where faith would lead her.

She strode into the office with the tattoo visible.

They started with catching up on where she had been while away. She shared more of the story than she did with Sister Angelica, since Maverick's past was now being resolved.

After hearing her tale, Pastor Flores asked for the events of the fair from her perspective. He listened with rapt attention, eyes wide as she described the struggle with Jason Waters.

"I'm just glad it ended as well as could be," she concluded.

"Amen to that. I've been messaging some of the area pastors the past few days. We're trying to decide how best to help the Waters family."

"It's going to be a hard legal battle for him," Vee said.

"It is," pastor agreed. "I don't see many ways for him to avoid jail time. I think the best we can do is collect money for Sister Waters and the children. Even though they were separated, he had joint custody. It will be hard on all of them."

Vee sighed. She tried not to think about the sad state of affairs. She could still see Jason Waters' face as he was taken away by police. That image, of a man entirely broken, stood out more to her than the violence and the fear from the attack.

"I pray they're able to find peace," she said finally. Though it was the only thing she could think to say, she truly meant it.

Pastor nodded, before tapping the desk with both hands.

"Yes, well, let's not dwell on the negatives. I asked you here today, sister Vee, for two reasons. First, this church owes you a huge 'thank you' for coordinating the county fair."

"You don't have to thank me," Viorica said, smiling. "In fact, you already did, during the Sunday service."

"Yes, but you are definitely deserving of it. After that one weekend, we've had more visitors than any other outreach event in the church. You made that happen, and I can't tell you how much I appreciate it."

Vee blushed at the words. "Glory to God," she said simply. "I just wanted to help."

"You have indeed." Pastor Flores came around his desk and sat in the armchair next to her. "Which brings me to my second point: besides owing you thanks, this church owes you...I owe you an apology."

Vee flinched. For a second, she forgot about the events of last year. She took it as a sign that she was doing well and growing beyond it.

"I try to do everything correctly," he went on. "Especially being a newer face to the church. There's a lot to juggle, but nothing really excuses the way things turned out. I dropped the ball, and it pushed you out of church. I'm sorry for that."

"I forgive you, Pastor," Vee said. Her voice was growing heavy again.

"Thank you, sister. But I don't mean to only offer a verbal apology. I would like to offer you a chance to be a part of Women's Ministry, in a leadership capacity. That is, if you're still interested?"

Vee nearly gasped. She opened her mouth to respond, but her thoughts became jumbled and ran together before she did.

Not long ago, that was her sole purpose in life. Hearing those words would have meant that she made it, that everything she had sown in sacrifice had finally produced a harvest.

It would have meant that God had given her vindication, she would have imagined.

Now, it was different, but so much more. She still had the desire, but it wasn't tied to her life's purpose any longer. She realized that she had plenty to live for, so if a position never came, she would still know that she was loved by God.

Her worth, and her pride, were no longer tied to the ministry. She wanted it, but she no longer needed it.

There was also the matter of the church rules, which served as her main objection.

"I would like that," she said. "But, there's a lot working against me right now. The church has a rule that people who leave and come back have to wait a year before serving in ministry. Last time, I only got six month in."

"That's true," Pastor Flores said, "but it's not specifically defined as a year. I read up on this one; the one-year statute is more of a guideline. The pastor is free to be flexible on that time limit. I think, with all we've seen, and how dedicated you've been, we can count what you've done as time served."

He smiled, and Vee started at his words.

"That's...what about my tattoo?"

She held out her arm for him to see. He waved a hand.

"Again, the pastor is free to rule on it. When you're speaking publicly, please just cover it up."

She took a deep breath. She had no more objections. This was really happening.

"if you say so...I'm in!" She broke out into a grin.

Pastor grinned in return, but then winced. "Oh! There's one more thing I forgot to mention!"

"What's that?" Vee asked, frowning. She felt like her heart was falling after flying so high.

"There's a small point of contention. The church rules make it tough to promote single people into positions of leadership. For a role as big as Women's Ministry, there are extra considerations in place."

Vee tried to keep the tremble out of her voice, and hated that she was failing. "What considerations are there? How soon can I clear them?"

Pastor shook his head. "There are extra steps. Lots of hoops to jump through. The ins and outs would take a while to navigate. I think there is a solution, though..."

Vee narrowed her eyes as he went to stand in the open doorway. She started to ask what was going on as anxiety skyrocketed.

She went catatonic on her feet as Archer walked through the door, in a black tuxedo.

His hair had been side-parted and the strands combed over. The black tux and crisp white dress shirt were dazzling, perfect in every square inch.

He smiled, wide, as he saw Viorica. He stood in front of her as her eyes blurred with tears, and a hand covered her mouth to hold back the sobs.

Archer addressed her, with a hand in his pocket.

"Viorica...Vee," he said, his voice low and satin-like. "A few days ago, I told you that I couldn't bring myself to stand in your way of being in ministry again. That was also the day I didn't know what was going to happen, and if we would be split apart again.

"All my life I've searched for a home, and people who feel like family to me. On that terrible day, I realized, out of everyone God has ever blessed me with by putting in my life, *you* are the one I couldn't live without, now that you're here."

Smoothly, he slid to one knee. At the same time, his hand came out of his pocket, holding a velvet box.

Vee gasped again, and her other hand went over her mouth, joining in keeping back the sobs. Out of the corner of her eye, she saw Pastor and Sister Flores in the doorway, grinning. Angelica was snapping pictures with her phone.

Archer opened the blue velvet box and held it up towards her. She was greeted by the fiery glint of a diamond-ladened gold band. It was beautiful, elegant in simplicity and stunning to behold.

"Viorica Iliescu," Archer said, voice thick with emotion. "I need you in my life. I cannot lose you. I don't want to spend a day without you. You are the best blessing God has placed in my life so far, and I love you with everything I am."

Vee somehow managed to extend a trembling hand.

Archer took her hand, enveloping her in warmth and security. Her trembling subsided.

"Will you marry me?" He asked in a husky whisper, fighting back tears.

She nodded, trying to find her words.

"Absolutely, yes," she said, furiously drying her eyes.

He slid the ring on her finger, and stood just in time for their second kiss.

Epilogue

Picture this: a mild spring day, in Ocala, Florida. In a lush green space within the heart of the city, an area has been manicured, roped off, and adorned with pristine white chairs and lace decorations.

A silk runner, dotted with flower petals, stretches across the partitioned lawn. The runner points to a soft carved wooden arch, adorned with leaves and strands of ivy. Behind the arch, the clear blue sky is visible, the sun drifting towards the horizon, bathing the area in a dreamlike golden glow.

Beneath the arch, next to Pastor Flores stands and a young man in a tuxedo, who has dreamt of home and family all his life. He sheds tears of thankfulness to God, knowing that the day has come.

Behind him are a line of gentlemen in black suits and powder blue ties. His best man, who has been like a brother to him since they were little, stands tall. Even with sunglasses, worn with permission to hide facial bruising, the best man cannot hide his falling tears.

Facing the groom are a line of women, adorned in custom-made powder blue silk dresses. Shalyn, the smallest, but still growing, stands at the head of the line. Followed behind her are Lois, Emma, Lisa, and Michelle, all grinning, and wiping tears of their own.

At the very front row of the audience sits the matron of honor, a frail but spiritually mighty woman, who has had the honor of serving as a surrogate mother to the bride. Next to her sits a tall, beautiful Italian woman, who has cried tears of joy every day for the past month, since being reunited with her daughter.

The wedding has just begun, and already there is not a dry eye to be found among the attendees.

Pastor Flores begins with a Scripture reading from the book of Psalms. He leads a prayer, thanking the God referenced in that Psalm, who is faithful to heal broken hearts, and bind up the wounds of those who are outcasts.

As he finishes, string and brass instruments begin to play, and everyone rises to their feet.

A beautiful young woman, who had been wounded, but has been restored, walks out the doorway of the church, and makes her way to the sectioned-off area.

A bald, Romanian man escorts her, holding his head high but letting his dignified tears fall. He, too, has been shedding tears every day for a month since reuniting with his daughter.

With her father on her arm, the young woman turns her face towards the sunset, towards the arch, striding confidently towards her God-given promise and future.

Author's Note

If, a handful of years ago, you had told me that I would publish not one, but *two* more books, I wouldn't have believed you. If you had told me that one of those books would be a romance novel, I probably would have laughed as I went my way.

But, if you had told me that the romance novel would be the one I'd been sitting on for years, that refused to leave me alone until it saw the light of day?

Well, not even I know what my reaction would have been.

Since the first day God formed this story in my soul, I never felt worthy of writing it to life. As you read this published work now, I wonder if I still feel unworthy. With 'Eastern Tales' I sort of beat myself up for delaying as long as I did. With this, I didn't feel that self-animosity; maybe it's spiritual growth, maybe it was Impostor Syndrome talking, but one thing's for sure: the season(s) of delay completely worked in my favor.

I had to rethink Shalyn from the ground up. Originally, her story was that of a young black girl sent to live with a relative because one parent was on drugs, and the other missing.

No, no, no.

Not again. Not anymore. Thank God for the delays, because I've reached the point where I'm tired of that being the narrative. That is the story recirculated throughout society for young black girls, and black people in general.

I don't care if it would have made for a better read. I don't care if audiences of other ethnicities find it more "believable" or "easier to empathize with". I don't even care if black audiences think it would be more relatable than the current story.

We are changing the narrative in life, so the least I can do is change it in fiction, and let art imitate life for a while.

Because we're tired of struggle. Tired of being defined by trauma.

It's time for all of us to rise.

I also had to reconsider the antagonists, Michelle and Emma (formerly 'Esmerelda'). I needed to rethink what exactly it was I wanted to get across with those characters. Before, they were pure adversaries, through-and-through.

Church rivalry does happen, but making their story a knockdown, drag out fight for ministry would have been a mistake.

Because what would that say about the state of Christianity? Had I left things as intended, it would have been completely unrealistic, and would not have served anyone. It also would have given opponents to the faith more ammunition, realistic or not. In order for us to truly get better, we have to understand where we are with one another, what the issue is, and from there work together for a solution.

Again, time for us *all* to rise.

This was difficult for me to balance how much self-insertion I wanted to have evident. More than anything, I need a tale that's entertaining, but I also need a tale that is believable. And with that comes the desire to show the truth of the struggle. I have been wounded in God's house, but I had to portray those scars without making a 1:1 retelling.

Maybe some will take exception to the story, for one reason or another. I can already imagine being called out for "airing dirty laundry"; but it's time to get the laundry clean. We are losing souls while we let dirty laundry linger. We all have to rise.

If you have a similar story, and have been wounded in God's house, this is for you. Connect with the story, empathize with the characters who face similar turmoil. Air the grief. Heal the wounds. And, most of all, find your way back into the arms of Jesus Christ.

Your steps are ordered, as well as your mistakes. Don't die alone on the sea of shame.

It's time for us all to rise. That includes you.

Come with us.

By faith

Chris H.